TANDEM BOOKS LIMITED

SAMY + LINDA

The Catch

John Boland

When Hogan Exe cut adrift the lifeless, caged
body of Hugh Hamilton, the monster trout in the
loch prepared to receive their seventeenth
victim. Hours earlier Hamilton had paid a large
sum for a choice stretch of the loch's fishing
rights . . .

Soon Jay Donaldson, a young American
millionaire, was to arrive at gaunt Aarolie
Castle. He too was to be offered an attractive
stretch of fishing on the loch. That the trout
themselves were bait used to ensnare wealthy
fishermen, Donaldson had no means of knowing.
But then the mysterious behaviour of the
castle's occupants cause him to hesitate; he
becomes aware of the owner's violent
temperament, his wierd and eccentric mother,
and his frighteningly un-balanced son.

The ever present tension mounts as Donaldson
probes the subdued but beautiful waitress, and
when he eventually stumbles on the macabre secret
of Aarolie it seems that he will become the next
horrible victim . . .

In THE CATCH John Boland has once again
demonstrated that for sheer ingenuity and
excitement of plot he is deservedly in the
forefront of to-day's thriller writers.

TO

PHILIPPA

The Catch

John Boland

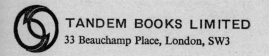
TANDEM BOOKS LIMITED
33 Beauchamp Place, London, SW3

First published in Great Britain by
George G. Harrap & Co. Ltd.

Copyright © John Boland

Tandem Edition 1965

Made and printed in Great Britain by
The Garden City Press Limited
Letchworth, Hertfordshire

Chapter One

HUGH HAMILTON stopped his car in order to consult the map once again. He stared in dismay at the red, brown and white squiggles that represented roads. He'd never been much good at map-reading and now it was impossible to decide which bit of squiggle he was on. Certainly this wasn't a main road; it was barely more than a track and the mountains became higher and the Scottish countryside wilder with every mile he went.

He was aching with tiredness and hunger. The scenery was beautiful, but it couldn't be eaten and he certainly wasn't going to sleep out in it. Not at his age. Not that he'd be able to sleep anyway—not unless he had a meal first. Opening the car door, he edged his ample body out on to the road, testing the ground at the side of it with his foot. As he suspected, the earth was wet, and boggy.

It was too soft to risk trying to turn the car; he'd have to drive on. After all, the road must run *somewhere*. There wasn't too much petrol in the tank either. Cursing, he got back in the car and drove off. A mile farther on he came to a T junction. There was no signpost and he tossed a coin to decide which way to go.

"Heads right, tails left." It came down tails, but after a short pause he turned right. No one, not even he himself, could ever say that Hugh Hamilton wasn't capable of making up his own mind.

And a mile farther on he knew he'd been correct in his choice. The road was following the contour of the mountainside, curving round it gently then running straight down into a shallow valley. Ahead, at the side of the road, there was a small cottage, and as he got nearer to it he saw a figure working in the tiny garden.

Thankfully, Hamilton pulled up at the cottage. "Is there an hotel hereabouts, my man?"

Tam Bruce raised his big frame slowly upright, eyeing the driver and the car's contents. The foreigner was a self-important-looking mannie, up for the fishing, judging from the tangle of equipment in the car.

"You'll be wanting Aarolie Castle," he said at last, ignoring the other man's impatience.

"Is that an hotel?"

"You're no' booked in there?"

Hamilton bit back the quick rebuke he was about to make. It was none of the man's business, but he would deal easily with him, otherwise the oaf might retaliate by misdirecting him. "No."

"Then you'll best be trying Aarolie. There isn'a anither hotel within thirty mile."

"How far is it?"

"Five mile."

"Then how do I get there?" His petrol wouldn't last more than fifteen or twenty miles.

"You'll keep straight on for two mile. Then there's a road to the left. You take that road and a piece on, half a mile, you'll be on a level stretch. There's a wood on your left and you'll see a gate and a wee bitty track. There's no'a sign, but the track leads up to the castle."

Hamilton repeated the instructions, then put the car into gear and was about to move off when his informant said: "Tell Hogan Exe—that's him at the castle—tell Mr. Exe that Tam Bruce sent you."

Tam Bruce watched the car shrink into the distance, then went slowly back to his cottage. He was a methodical man and before he did anything else he made a note about the stranger. He, Tam, would be calling in at Aarolie to collect the dram Mr. Exe gave him for any visitor steered to the hotel. If he didn't make a note, he might forget. Bruce looked at his watch. It was almost time to begin his tour of duty and he stripped off his gardening clothes. After a brief cold-water wash he began to dress again, this time in the uniform of a constable.

Although Hamilton wasn't any good at map-reading, he was able to follow Bruce's instructions without difficulty. The wood was a plantation of spruce and half-way along it he saw the gate, open and apparently never used, for there was a cattle grid let into the track to prevent the passage of animals.

The track led in a gentle curve through the trees and then, abruptly, he was through the wood and in the open, with Aarolie Castle about a hundred and fifty yards ahead. Even Hamilton was impressed. The huge, granite structure stood at the entrance to a glen, at the end of a tongue of rock that jutted into the waters of a loch.

Surrounding the castle was a curtain of mountains that ranged along on either side and came down to the edge of the water on the far shore, dropping sheer into the loch at one point; the peaks reflected in the calm surface. It was a scene that must have been unchanged for centuries. Hundreds of years ago it was perhaps the stronghold of a chieftain and the site of bloody battles in the clan wars.

Today, although it seemed peaceful enough, there was an air of menace about the place, it was becoming colder, the sun disappeared behind the mountains; but as he drove up to the entrance Hamilton laughed at himself. He needed a drink—several drinks—and a meal. That'd soon put paid to his stupid jitters.

As he climbed stiffly from the driver's seat he peered up at the sign, a huge board erected ten or twelve feet in the air on an oak column. The gaudily painted scene depicted two gigantic trout that were angling. They each had a puny man hooked and were apparently trying to land them. Under this unlikely picture was the title: THE MONSTERS OF THE

GLEN. He was still looking up at it when he heard a deep voice, with an English accent.

"Good evening, sir."

Hamilton turned to look at the speaker, who had come out silently from the castle entrance and was standing a couple of yards away, motionless. He was a big man, very big, in shirt sleeves, about fifty, with a black beard that was beginning to turn grey.

"Have you a room for the night?" The words came out more abruptly than Hamilton intended, but he'd been startled by the man's appearance from nowhere. "A man called Bruce said you might have."

"Tam Bruce?"

"That's right."

"Then of course we must find a room for you, sir." The bearded man smiled, but to Hamilton there was no warmth in it; Exe—if that was who he was—was looking at him as though wondering if the newcomer should be admitted— whether he looked acceptable. Hamilton flushed. By heck, there was nothing wrong with him, nor his credit! Now he'd sold the store, he was, not to put too fine a point on it, a comfortable man.

"You'll be Mr. Exe?"

"That's right. I'm the proprietor." He moved forward. "Let me help you with your baggage, Mr. . . . ?"

"Hamilton."

"We're rather short of assistance here, Mr. Hamilton, but I think we'll be able to make you comfortable." He opened the boot of the car and lifted the big leather trunk with one hand as though it were empty. The fat man's lips tightened. Even with both hands he could barely manage to shift that case; it had been a mistake to bring it.

Hamilton trotted behind the big man, panting. They crossed the gravel and entered the castle. Inside, the hall was enormous, dwarfing the desk beside the door, which was apparently used for reception purposes. The flagged floor seemed as big as a tennis court, with a huge, winding staircase on the far side.

Exe put down the trunk and went to the desk, opening the Registration Book. "Mr. Hamilton, if you'd sign this?" He regarded his guest while the other man wrote his signature and home address. "From the Midlands, I see."

"That's right."

"Will you be staying long, sir?"

"Depends on the fishing." He gave a nervous laugh. His host's piercingly blue eyes were regarding him in an odd manner: it made him feel cold.

"We have the finest fishing in Britain, sir. Perhaps the best in the world."

"That's a big claim, Mr. Exe. Too big, I'd say." There was a moment's silence then Hamilton shuffled uncomfortably. "If I could see the room?"

"But of course, sir. Leave your cases here; my son will bring them up to your room. And don't bother about your car either; if you'll leave the key I'll see it's put away." Exe led the way towards the staircase. "I'm afraid we haven't got a lift, sir, but the room's on the first floor."

After the vastness of the entrance-hall the corridor was narrow, the room cramped. But at least it was clean enough and the bed looked comfortable. The proprietor stood in the doorway watching Hamilton make a quick examination of the room. "Will this be suitable?"

"It'll do."

"Excellent. . . . I'll go down and see about a meal for you, sir. I dare say you could manage something to eat?" He smiled again, as though at some private joke. "Our other guests finished dinner some time ago, but we'll be able to get you something. . . . Shall we say in ten minutes, sir? I'll be waiting in the entrance-hall." He was still smiling as he closed the door.

Hamilton shivered. Somehow the place struck him as being cold . . . and Exe was a damned sight colder, even with all his politeness. There was something about those incredible eyes . . .! Despite the fact that Hogan Exe was English, it was easy enough to picture him in Highland dress, leading his clan into battle, but the plain fact was that he sounded slightly common. Hamilton had spent a lifetime in placing people's accents and he could always tell when someone was common.

"Damn and blast!" Only the cold-water tap worked. There wasn't even a dribble from the other one, but before he could swear again there was a knock on the door. "Come in!" The complaint he'd been about to make was stifled. One of the staff came in. She was a pale, repressed-looking little blonde; the dowdy clothes she wore almost obscured the fact that she was beautiful. She was carrying a towel-covered jug.

"I've brought you some hot water, sir." She put the jug down by the basin and was gone before he could think of anything to say to her. Mebbe it wasn't going to be so bad here after all! She'd got a right good figure. Nice legs, too. He was very partial to a well-shaped leg.

He looked at his reflection in the mirror. "Mebbe some good sport hereabouts, Hughie, eh?" He turned sideways, pulling in his belly. Standing like that he was a fine figure of a man; mature, of course, but well preserved.

When he got down into the entrance-hall the gigantic proprietor was waiting to show him the way to the dining-room. "Did my niece bring you some hot water?"

So she was the boss's niece! That made it a bit more chancy. "Yes, thank you." He walked into the dining-room as the proprietor held the door open. It was smaller than he'd expected, with a dozen tables, all of them empty.

"How many other guests are there?"

"Half a dozen, sir, at the moment."

Exe pulled back a chair at a table near the huge window. "There's a fine view from here." He pushed the chair in as

10

Hamilton settled his bulk. "I'm afraid we've not got much variety in the way of food, but if you've no objection to a broth, then perhaps some fresh salmon?"

"That's fine."

"Anything to drink?"

He was going to order a lager but thought better of it. It was as well to establish that he wasn't just any casual guest. "You've champagne?" It was precisely the right attitude to take and he congratulated himself. Exe paused for a moment, as though taken aback, and then became even more attentive. "I'll bring you the bottle myself, sir."

The big man bowed and hurried away, obviously impressed.

Hamilton nodded to himself, satisfied, then was even more pleased when the green-baize covered service doors swung open and the blonde entered, bringing his first course. He was hungry and was spooning the broth up almost before she'd put the bowl on the table. Time enough after he'd eaten to get to know her.

From the first scalding mouthful Hamilton realized the broth had been made by a master hand. No one could fool him about the quality of food—or wine. Imagine a dead hole like this having '53 champagne! By the time he'd finished the meal he was in what was, for him, a mellow mood. He was having his brandy when Exe came into the dining-room and over to his table.

"I trust you enjoyed your dinner, sir?"

"Not bad. Not bad at all."

"Would you care to have another brandy, sir? On the house, as it were?"

"I wouldn't say no." He never did, to anything free.

"Then perhaps you'd like to come and have it in my office."

Hogan Exe's office was oddly mixed. Two of the panelled walls were covered with bookshelves packed with volumes; the other two walls were also covered—but with stuffed

11

fish in glass cases. The light was dim and for a moment Hamilton thought the fish were salmon. But then he looked closer and gaped.

"Trout! *That* size?"

Exe nodded. "The Monsters of the Glen, sir."

"Good God! " In the forty years he'd been a fisherman, the fat man had never seen anything like the specimens in the cases, not one of which was under sixteen pounds. But then his habitual caution returned. "They're fakes! "

The other man's eyes glittered weirdly in the light. "You won't say that after you've caught one yourself, Mr. Hamilton."

"You really mean there are *still* fish like that? Here?"

"If you're anything of a fisherman, sir, I guarantee to show where there's one of the monsters to be killed."

Hamilton flopped into a chair, unable to believe his good fortune. Stumbling on a place like this—an obscure, unknown fisherman's paradise! He watched Exe pour out a very large brandy, then take one himself. "Shall we drink to it?"

Exe cradled the glass in his hand, swilling the brandy round and round. "When you've seen what the sport is like, Mr. Hamilton, I hope you'll stay with us for a time. . . . Unless, of course, you have to get back to business?"

"Nay. No business for me. Not any longer. I've retired, sold out." Exe looked interested and once again Hamilton congratulated himself. Here was someone actually inviting Hugh Hamilton to tell the story of the successful life and career of Hugh Hamilton. It had been a long time since he'd had the opportunity.

"So I'm me own boss, you see. Always have been, of course, but it's different now. No responsibility."

"Very nice too." Exe sighed. "I wish I could make enough money to retire. . . But I'm not smart enough."

His guest considered the statement judicially, head cocked to one side. "You're right, of course. You've got to be smart

12

in business. Believe me, I know. There was a dozen blokes would have liked to stab me in the back, but I was a damn sight smarter than them."

He raised no objection to the further measure of brandy which his host poured out, settling himself a little more comfortably in the leather armchair as he launched into his story. By the time he had finished the tale his opinion of the bearded man had been revised. Exe was a capital chap; he hadn't interrupted once, except to make admiring murmurs—a thing that had never happened before in all the many, many times that Hamilton had forced his life story on a listener—or that version of it which he cared to pass on.

"You've had a remarkable life, Mr. Hamilton," Exe said at last. "Remarkable! "

"I've worked for it, mister. Worked for forty-six years." He emptied his glass. "And now I'm going to enjoy life. I can afford to."

Exe was still shaking his head in admiration. "I take my hat off to you, sir, I really do. . . . Would you mind if I introduced you to my Mother? She'd be delighted to meet you, and she'll be free now. Mother does the cooking."

Hamilton had taken it for granted that the cook was a chef, but he had no objection to meeting the woman. "A damn fine cook if I may say so." He was surprised by the quick movement with which Exe rose to his feet and smiled at someone standing behind Hamilton.

"Hello, Mother, I was just talking about you."

Hamilton twisted his neck to look, but couldn't see and reluctantly dragged himself up on his feet. It wasn't in his scale of social behaviour to stand up when a mere cook entered the room, but in this place everything seemed queer. And the sight of Mrs. Exe was the oddest thing yet.

She was dressed in Elizabethan costume.

Mrs. Mary Exe was elderly and cottage-loaf shaped. Her round body was clad in a garb that might have been suitable for a fancy-dress ball. She held out a regal hand and for a moment Hamilton had the absurd impression that he was supposed to kiss it.

"How—how do you do."

She smiled on him, a maternal, pleasant-faced old woman, with eyes that were a pale replica of her son's. "We hope you will enjoy your stay, Mr. Hamilton," she said after the introductions had been made. Hamilton was uncertain whether she was referring to her son and herself, or using the royal "we."

She was probably a bit senile, although she looked shrewd enough, and she certainly knew how to cook. She knocked back the brandy Hogan poured for her with alarming speed then went to the door. "We shall see you in the morning, Mr. Hamilton."

The moment she had gone he had the feeling that she had never been there—that her appearance had been an hallucination. The fumes of brandy were filling his head; none of that evening's experiences seemed quite real, but when he opened his eyes and stared round the panelled office again there was no doubting the existence of the giant trout in the glass cases.

"You must forgive my Mother her little hobby, sir. I hope she didn't scare you, dressed up like that?" Exe was smiling easily. "Mother has a fine collection of period costumes and she likes to wear one or two of them now and again—she says it keeps them aired."

"Yes. Yesh, of course." Hamilton was aware that his tongue was becoming difficult to control; it was time for bed. He yawned. "Well, I think it's time I went up to my room."

"Of course." Exe was on his feet, moving towards the door. "I enjoyed our chat, Mr. Hamilton. We must talk again. But for tonight—I hope you sleep well. All our other guests do; they never hear a sound."

Hamilton yawned again. It was certainly excellent brandy that the bearded man served. "Good night."

"Good night, sir."

As the fat man climbed the staircase he paused for a moment. In the silence he could hear his own heart-beats thudding. The quietness was so complete he might have been standing in a tomb. He shivered. In the dim light that partly illuminated the great hall he fancied he could see figures, people standing just on the edge of the shadows, watching him.

There was just one oil-lamp alight in the corridor, its flickering flame throwing more shadows, and he was glad to hurry back from the w.c. into his bedroom. He shut the door and bolted it, letting out a puffing sigh of relief. The three-inch-thick oak would keep him safe from whatever was moving in the corridor.

His suitcase had been opened and his pyjamas laid out on the downturned bed, his slippers arranged neatly, ready to be stepped into. The comforting sight enabled him to shake off some of the apprehension that had crowded in on him. No doubt about it, these old castles had an atmosphere that could almost be *felt*. Hamilton belched, then patted his stomach. He'd have to take a stomach powder in order to sleep; the salmon and the cheese he'd eaten . . . maybe he'd taken a mite more than he should have.

He mixed the draught and went to stand at the open window, taking in deep breaths. Even the air was heady, the smell of the water filled the room and when he tried to peer down over the thick sill he drew back in alarm; he hadn't realized that it was a sheer drop from the window to the surface of the loch forty feet below.

The window shut, he began to undress, taking off his shoes. Should he put them outside the door? But nothing would persuade him to open it again tonight, short of the place catching fire. Plumping down on the bed, he thrust his feet into the slippers, then gave a yelp of pain. Something had hurt his right foot. Gingerly he took off the slipper and stared aghast at the No. 4 trout-hook that was sticking in the sole of his foot.

Fortunately it had only just penetrated the skin; the barb hadn't caught. If he'd been standing up when he put his foot in the slipper, with his weight on it . . . It made him sick to think of what would have happened.

But how in the name of hell had the hook got there?

Chapter Two

HAMILTON spent a bad night, jerking awake the moment he dropped off to sleep, roused by what sounded like someone in the room chuckling. There was a wind blowing across the loch and the noise was probably caused by the water slapping against the bottom of the castle wall.

It was a relief when finally he heard someone knock on the door and try the handle. The girl's voice called out: "I've left your shaving water, sir." But by the time he had scrambled out of bed and unbolted the door, she was gone, leaving the towel-covered copper jug on the mat, outside.

With the dawn the wind had died and now there was a mist on the water. Somewhere in the distance he could hear the B.B.C. accent of a newsreader, but then the radio was switched off and again he realized how silent the place was.

Breakfast was served by the blonde, who coped with the half-dozen men, each one of whom sat at a separate table. She moved quickly and gracefully, attending to the guests, but seemed to be doing the work mechanically, as though her thoughts were far away.

Only one of the other men gave a brief nod to Hamilton; the rest ignored him, concentrating on their breakfast with almost ferocious attention as they hurried to get the meal over so that they could get out on the real business of life; killing fish.

Hamilton was the last one to leave the dining-room and as he stepped into the hall, Hogan Exe greeted him. "You'll be ready, Mr. Hamilton?"

"In fifteen minutes."

"Then I'll see you outside."

The fat man nodded and went plodding up the stairs to

his room. Where did the other guests sleep? The room he occupied was the only one he'd seen—there was no other door in the corridor, except those leading to the bathroom and the w.c. More to the point—where did the girl sleep? The castle was big enough to accommodate a hundred people, maybe more.

Did she have a room round the corner? It would do no harm to have a look at the farther corridor. Beyond the bathroom the passage ran for another three or four yards, then turned off at right-angles. The moment he turned the corner he halted abruptly. The entire passage was boarded up.

So only part of the castle was in use. Out of curiosity he retraced his steps to the top of the staircase and went on in the opposite direction. He passed six doors before a bend in the corridor revealed the passage ahead to be boarded up completely. Six doors and his own—did that mean that there were seven rooms for guests? If it were so, how the devil could Exe run the place without making a tremendous loss?

He went back to his own room and saw, on the dressing-table, the No. 4 trout-hook that had been in his slipper the previous night. How it had got into his slipper was a mystery and now he had remembered the incident his foot began to give pain. He'd take the hook out to the car and make sure it was safe with the rest of his gear.

Outside the air was still and warm. He turned right, looking for the garage. It must be in that direction; the loch waters were on the other side. Round the corner of the massive wall a lean-to shed had been built, large enough to house a dozen cars. The doors were open and he could see his own vehicle in front. Someone had got the bonnet up and was stooped over, apparently examining the engine.

"What are you doing!"

The overalled figure straightened and stood towering over Hamilton. "Morning Admiral, sir. Your boat's got a sweet power plant."

Hamilton stared up at the other person, his face going blotched with anger. The stranger looked ridiculous. Well over six feet tall, round-faced and with a few wispy hairs on his upper lip, he was perhaps seventeen. His eyes were wide set and staring and his mouth was stretched in a grin. What made him look so incongruous was the fact that above the overalls he wore a naval rating's hat, with a decorative band that, instead of giving the name of one of H.M. ships, commanded that, apparently, all and sundry should: *Kiss me quick, love.*

It was the youth's eyes that made Hamilton swallow his wrath. They were regarding him steadily with a queer intensity, and although they were a darker blue they were very like those of Hogan Exe.

"Are—are you Mr. Exe's son?"

"Yes. I'm Willie."

"I see. Well, I didn't order any work to be done on my car, so you can close the bonnet."

"It's a beautiful job." One large hand was stroking the radiator, almost as though he was caressing it. "I'm going to have a car like this myself, one of these days."

"No doubt." Hamilton's voice was sharp with irony. "All you need to do is to save a few thousand pounds and then you'll be able to buy one."

"Oh, I'll not buy it. Dad will give me one."

"Yes, I'm sure he will."

For the first time the grin left the youth's face. "I'll be getting on with my work." He leaned forward as though to whisper and Hamilton stepped away quickly, faintly alarmed. "I'm building a ship, a secret ship," Willie confided. Without another word he went striding off, marching as though on a parade ground, arms swinging and chin up.

Hamilton wiped the sweat from his face. The lad was batty, like his grandmother. He'd have included Hogan Exe in that category, except for the gigantic fish trophies in the office. They were no fisherman's fiction.

He closed the bonnet and opened the driver's door to get the special pouch in which he kept his fishing-hooks. It was kept in a separate compartment under the dashboard and as he reached in to get it he saw something glinting under his nose. Another hook, this time a No. 6, was caught in the folds of leather on the driving seat. If he'd climbed in behind the wheel the hook would have gone straight into the back of his thigh.

Shaken, he turned to look for Willie, but the big youth had disappeared from sight. Had Willie put the hooks where they might have caused damage? But no, that was fantastic. He hadn't even met the youth when the hooks had been left. No, it must have been an accident, although how had it happened . . . ?

"Are you ready, sir?"

Hogan's deep voice startled him. He hadn't heard the bearded man approach. Exe had a wicker basket in one hand. "My Mother's put you up a lunch, sir. I think you'll find there's plenty." He stared at Hamilton, then at the car. "I saw my boy coming from here a moment ago. . . . Was he looking at the engine?"

"How did you know?"

Exe laughed. "He's very keen on car engines, Mr. Hamilton, and it isn't very often he sees such an expensive car as yours. . . . He doesn't mean any harm." The statement was made flatly, without a hint of expecting sympathy for his unfortunate son, and Hamilton dropped the subject with a warning.

"So long as he doesn't do any damage."

This time Exe's laughter was loud. "Bless you, sir, Willie wouldn't harm an *engine*. He loves 'em too much. You can take it from me, sir, if Willie did anything to an engine, then that engine would be all the better for what he did. Willie's a brilliant boy in that respect. Engines, electrical gadgets—that sort of thing. You should see what he's made. . . . But there, we don't want to waste time, do we? If you're ready, sir?"

They went to the water's edge where a heavy rowing-boat was tied up. Exe held the boat steady while his guest got in, then cast off and began to row. Hamilton watched the smooth actions; the other man's sleeves were rolled up high and the play of muscles in his arms fascinated the older man.

The boat was cutting through the water as though it was being propelled by an engine, but Exe's strength made it all look effortless. They were out of sight of the land now, cut off by the mist, but the rower didn't hesitate. "I'm taking you to a spot where you should kill a fair-sized fish or two."

"If there's fish in the water, then I'll hook 'em."

Hamilton had never known a day like it. The burn must have been alive with fish. On his very first cast something that felt like an express train attached itself to the hook and within seconds the line had parted. His arms felt as though they were being wrenched out of their sockets, but the lust for sport overcame everything—even food.

Long before Exe returned to pick him up, Hamilton gave up. He would need much stronger tackle to deal with the monsters in the water. Indeed, it would need salmon-fishing equipment if he was going to land some of the really big ones. For his day's sport he had only two trout to show— but what trout they were; both of them more than twice the size of anything he had ever netted before.

He greeted Exe with delight, and didn't stop telling the hotelier of the day's experiences all the way back to the castle. Fifty yards short of the shore, Exe stopped rowing, letting the boat drift. "You'll be staying on then, I take it?"

"You won't be able to drive me away!" Hamilton suffered a twinge of caution. Better not sound too enthusiastic, the feller might put up the hotel charges.

Hogan was resting on his oars, studying the other man closely.

"Mr. Hamilton," he said at last, "I think you're a real fisherman." His passenger kept silent, wondering what was coming. "Yes, a real fisherman, a real sportsman. I wonder if you'll be likely to come here again, next year, say?"

"Why?"

"I might have a proposition to put to you. Only might, mark you." Hogan's forehead wrinkled in perplexity. "Maybe we should have another little chat tonight, in my office?"

"What about?"

"I'd like to talk fishing."

What the devil did the chap mean? But did it matter? Hamilton remembered the line-breaking pulls he had suffered and was filled with the glow of glorious achievement. Just as soon as he could get the proper tackle he'd be into a giant fish that would send the mayor, and the rest of the boys back home, green with envy.

Without saying anything more, Exe rowed to the shore and took Hamilton's fish to be weighed correctly. The larger one was a fraction of an ounce over five pounds, but compared with the huge fish in the glass cases in the panelled office, they were minnows.

"I'll get Mother to cook one of these for your dinner, sir."

"Right. I'll go for a bath, if there's hot water?"

"Yes, sir, plenty."

The bath was too narrow for a man of Hamilton's generous build, but on this day of days he was in too good a temper to allow such a thing to upset him. When he got back to his room, however, he frowned. He'd put his wallet on the *right*-hand side of the dressing-table; he remembered distinctly putting it down. But now it was on the other side.

He checked through its contents, but nothing was missing. He always knew to a penny how much cash he carried and the total value of stamps. Had the girl been in and gone through it, putting the thing down without taking any money? Did she want to check if he had plenty of money? Or had that great lumpkin, Willie, been in the room?

Anyway there was no harm done. Now he knew, every time he left the bedroom he would take his wallet with him. He laughed. At least there weren't any more fish-hooks strewn round the place.

By the time he went down to dinner he'd forgotten the incident and the trout was so delicious he never thought to watch Selina to see if she reacted in a suspicious manner; he had meant to stare at her and note any expression of guilt. The man who had nodded to him at breakfast was a little more forthcoming, asking him if he'd had a good day's sport.

"I dare say you'll be coming again, now you've found the place? I've been coming for three years." He leaned across confidentially. "You're honoured, if you did but know it. Hogan's very particular who he has as his guests."

"You mean he doesn't take everyone in?"

"Too true he doesn't. Very selective, friend Exe."

It was something to think over. The only solution seemed to be that Exe was, in his way, as batty as the other members of his family. A place like this should be a gold-mine. Instead of seven guests, there should be seventy.

But after dinner, in the panelled dimness of Hogan Exe's office, Hamilton was given the reason.

"I want this place to be exclusive, Mr. Hamilton," Exe told him. "You know, have just a few selected members. Of course, if it's going to be kept that way, it'll need paying for." He was striding up and down, his movements uncannily quiet. "So, on the one hand, the members would have to be rich men, and they'd have to be acceptable."

"Go on."

"On the other hand, they'd have to keep quiet about the fishing, otherwise we'd be swamped. There's a limit to the numbers of fish, sir, so our club members must be the type who'd keep their mouths shut, their tongues silent."

There was something peculiar in Exe's manner as he spoke the last few words. This wasn't just a straight account of a situation; there was something behind it all, something Hamilton couldn't quite grasp.

"It costs a great deal of money to keep this place going," Hogan said significantly. "I want to raise the standard of comfort, but it's a long job. Even if you've had a good year, there isn't much cash left by the time you've paid taxes and everything."

Now Hamilton understood where the conversation had been leading. "Aye, taxes!" he replied feelingly. "They'd skin you alive, the Inland Revenue."

"You're a man of understanding, Mr. Hamilton," Exe said gravely. He poured out another measure of brandy for them both. "If you're going to make a profit at all, you've got to be careful with the bookkeeping. Of course, if you're dealing with cash sales . . . !" His piercingly blue eyes regarded the fat man over the rim of his glass.

Hamilton settled back in his chair, very sure of himself. He'd struck deals of this kind many times and somehow it reduced Exe in stature. He was no longer the rather scarifying figure of a Highland pirate, but merely a dishonest man trying to make a fast buck. "All right, Exe, what's the deal?"

If it was possible for a man of Hogan's build to cringe, he was doing so now. "I—I sell members a private stretch of water."

"How much?"

"Twelve hundred pounds. Cash."

Any other man might have reeled at the sum, but not Hamilton. He gazed across at one of the glass cases. According to the label the specimen inside it weighed 20 lb. 3 oz. and it had been taken in the glen last year. By God, if he could land such a monster . . . !

"Well, sir?"

"You've got yourself another member, Exe, providing you can assure me on a few points." Hamilton had spent a lifetime in competitive trade and he was no fool. Before he forked out a penny piece he'd be sure that everything was in order. "First, where's this stretch of water you're proposing to sell me?"

From his desk, Hogan took out a large-scale map and unrolled it to show the other man. Hamilton was no good at maps, but he could understand this one. It showed a mile or so of river, with red lines drawn across it at intervals and in the centre of each section a red star with a name lettered in beside it.

"Those the blokes that own the various pieces?"

"Yes."

The guest peered at the names, but he didn't know any of them. Only two of the sections weren't marked. "Only two pieces left?"

"There's another river, when this one is finished."

Hamilton scratched his head. Twelve hundred pounds was a lot of money to pay. Would it be worth it? From what the bearded man said next he might have been reading Hamilton's mind.

"It's a lot of money, but there's more to it than just a stretch of water. We fix up a room—your own, private room, so you can stay when and as long as you like, during the season."

"Done."

An hour later, Hogan went into the kitchen in search of his Mother. Tonight she was dressed as Queen Victoria and sitting at the gigantic work-table as though conducting a council of her Ministers of Government. "I think Mr. Hamilton is going to join the Club, Mother."

Mrs. Exe smiled vaguely, intent on preparing a shopping-list. "That will be nice, dear, if you're sure he's the sort of man you want."

Her son considered the matter carefully. "I think so," he said at last. "He's rich, retired and a widower. No family to bother about, no one to worry about him if he keeps the trout company."

"Noodles."

"I beg your pardon?"

"Noodles, dear. We've run out. Willie must get some when you send him shopping."

She peered round the huge, vaulted kitchen, trying to think if there was anything else she wanted, then became aware that her son was staring at her patiently. "Oh, hello, dear, did you want something?"

"I was talking about Mr. Hamilton, Mother. Mr. Hamilton, who's going to join our Club."

"Why, that's splendid, Hoagy."

"You've got nothing against him, Mother?"

"Good gracious no. Poor lonely soul. . . . He's rather fat, but that's a good thing, isn't it?"

"Do you agree he joins?"

"Of course, dear boy. Anything you say. You know Mother relies on your judgment." She raised a finger. "Nuts! " Painstakingly she wrote down the word "Nuts" on the shopping-list that was beside the menu cards and promptly forgot Hogan's presence. After a moment he shrugged, leaving her to her task. Mother took her work very seriously.

There was no one about, the guests had all retired for the night and he had the place to himself for the time being. He strode out into the night and stood looking out over the water. It thrilled him every time he saw it, and especially at night.

He stood there wondering if he'd been right to ask twelve hundred from Hamilton; it seemed likely that the fat old man might have paid more. But it was too late to do anything about it now; the deal was made. Hogan cocked his head to listen and heard the faint sound of bicycle tyres

26

on the gravel of the drive.

"That you, Tam?"

"Good evening to you, Master Exe."

The constable's figure loomed up in the darkness and Exe smiled to himself. "You'll be looking for poachers, no doubt."

"Have you seen hide or hair?" Tam asked eagerly.

"Nothing."

"Ah, man! But they're here. I can feel it in me bones. They're here, the devils!"

"I've not seen any strangers in the glen, Tam."

"Ah, well 'tis my job to lay them by the heels." He paused, then went on delicately: : "And how's the trade with you, sir? Flourishin', I trust?"

"Not bad, not bad." He drew in his breath sharply. "I hadn't realized there was such a bite in the air."

"Oh, aye, 'tis cool enough, no doubt."

"You've a long way to go, Tam. Would you take a dram to keep the cold out?"

Tam gave it judicial consideration, then accepted. The proprieties had been observed and he could afford to relax. "A medicinal droppie, if you would, Master Exe, and thank ye for being so considerate o' ma health."

Ten minutes later Tam cycled off with three generous whiskies under his belt. "I'll no light ma lamp whilst I'm on your land, sir. It's no committing an offence and I might trap the poachers."

As the sound of the tyres faded, a new noise made itself heard—that of an electric drill being used in the lean-to. Hogan smiled. Willie was busy working on the space ship.

Chapter Three

HAMILTON drew the money for the fishing rights from a bank forty miles away in order to allay Exe's fear that the cash might be traced to Aarolie Castle. It took several days for the money to be transferred and by the time he was able to put through the transaction, Hamilton was in a sweat of fear in case Exe withdrew the offer.

So far Hamilton hadn't landed a real giant, but a fourteen-pound fish had whetted his appetite. Even Selina was temporarily forgotten; at his age, the retired draper found he had energy for only one pursuit at a time.

He got back to the castle in time for dinner and carried the suitcase with the money inside into the dining-room, afraid to let it out of his sight. Somehow he'd expected the bearded man to be waiting to welcome him back, but Exe was missing.

"Is your uncle in his office?" he asked Selina.

"I think he's out with one of the gentlemen, sir."

The hotel proprietor still hadn't shown up by the time Hamilton had finished dinner and the fat man left the dining-room, wondering what to do. He didn't want to be burdened with so much cash. Really, it was too bad!

He went back into the dining-room and beckoned Selina. "The moment your uncle returns, tell him I'll be in my room."

"Very good, sir." She sounded tired.

But when he got up to his room and opened the door he had a shock. Everything of his had been taken out and the bed stripped down to the mattress. Sudden fear made the hairs on the back of his neck prickle. He clutched the suitcase to his chest almost as though someone was trying

28

to snatch it from him, then wheeled in fresh alarm as a deep voice sounded behind him.

"I'm sorry, sir. Willie forgot to tell you." Hogan Exe was standing just a yard away, his eyes bright.

"Did—didn't tell me what?" The words were gasped; Hamilton's heart was still thumping from shock.

"That we've given you another room, sir." Exe shook his head in annoyance. "There now, the very evening I wanted everything to go smoothly, and Willie forgets!" He smiled placatingly. "I do hope you'll forgive me, sir. But you see, as a new club member I thought we'd better put you into a better room."

Hamilton was laughing now. The noise he was making was tinged with hysteria. For a dreadful moment he'd thought . . . ! But Hogan's firm hand was gripping his elbow and he felt himself propelled out of the room and along the corridor towards the staircase, past it and into the stretch of passageway that Hamilton had explored previously.

Outside one of the oak doors Exe halted. "Your new room, sir. I hope you like it."

The fat man entered and had a job to keep himself from gaping. His pyjamas were laid out on a four-poster bed that was the main piece of furniture in the panelled room, which was six times as large as the one he had just left. Brightly coloured rugs scattered on the floor added vivid touches to the place and the log fire in the enormous hearth, two winged armchairs in front of it, gave an atmosphere of cheerfulness.

"It's a magnificent room."

"It's the way I want to get all of them, sir, when I've got the money."

Money. He became aware that he was still clutching the small case as though he expected it to be torn from his grasp at any moment. But Exe was pointing out various features of the room. "Bathroom through that door—the

29

other doors lead into the wardrobe." He became brisk.
"Now, sir, if you'd like to get ready for bed, I'll bring the
papers up, you can sign them and we'll all be happy."

Hamilton nodded. Exe was doing things in the right
order. There'd be no handing over of cash until *after* the
signatures had been put on the document. "Right. Just
give me ten minutes."

The bearded man returned, prompt to the second, bringing with him not only the documents to be signed, but a
bottle filled with clear liquid, and two glasses. Hamilton,
in pyjamas and dressing-gown, read the wording of the
papers he had to sign, grunted his approval and scribbled
his signature, then nodded to the small suitcase, on the
table beside the bed.

"The money's all there. Do you want to check it?"

"Good heavens, sir, of course not!" Hogan's teeth shone
in the darkness of his beard. "I know when I can trust
someone!" He held up the bottle. "How about sealing the
deal, sir?" He moved forward, confidentially. "This is the
real Highland malt. One hundred proof! You can't buy
it at any price. One drop of this and you sleep like a
babe."

He poured out two small tots and handed one glass to
the other man. "Long life and prosperity!"

"Here's to a thirty-pounder!"

Hamilton sipped at the liquid. It lay on his tongue peace-
fully, docile as milk, but when he swallowed it he felt it
glowing warm and powerful as it went down his throat.
For a moment he couldn't get his breath. The stuff had
the kick of a carthorse whose hoof was padded with velvet.

"Bottoms up!"

"Bottoms up!" He drained the glass and this time got
the full effect of the stuff. Exe hadn't blinked an eyelid;
he must have rhinocerous hide lining his stomach. The
fat man felt momentarily dizzy, something had gone wrong
with his eyesight, he couldn't focus on anything. Exe's

face was advancing and receding in alarming fashion and then became a ball of whitish mist.

"Steady on, old man!"

Hamilton felt an arm go round his waist—an arm iron-hard with muscle, then he was being carried. Exe laid him out on the four-poster, smiling, then consulted his wrist-watch. When Hamilton was asleep and breathing stertorous-ly, Hogan nodded.

"Good."

Leaving the bedside, he walked over to the far side of the fireplace where he fumbled with the panelling for a moment before sliding a small portion of it to one side. In the recess that was revealed there was a telephone and two differently coloured buttons; he pressed the red one.

Willie Exe heard the buzzer and looked up. Above the work bench there was a glass panel with the words "Action Stations" painted on it. Behind the glass an electric light bulb flicked on and off, illuminating the sign.

He gave a salute. "Aye, aye, Captain."

Putting down the screwdriver he had been using, he went out from the rear of the lean-to and into the castle. Granny was in the kitchen, reading a book. She gave a wild shriek as he stole up behind her and hooted with mad laughter almost in her ear.

"Oh, Willie, you naughty boy!" One hand was at her throat as she tried to steady her breathing. "You frightened me half to death."

"Didn't you hear the Captain calling?"

"Calling?" she said vaguely. "I've got a new knitting pattern. You could do with another sweater, dear, for the colder weather."

"Granny!" he pleaded. "There's the intercom."

"The what, dear?"

"Oh, Granny! The intercom. . . . You know."

"Oh, that telephone you put in." She cocked her head

to listen. "Yes, I can hear it. What a very clever boy you are to be sure!"

He was almost dancing with impatient rage. "Aren't you going to answer it?"

"Don't get so impatient, dear, it isn't good for you." Beaming fondly at him, she got stiffly to her feet and went across to a wall cupboard marked "Oatmeal." Opening the door, she took out the telephone handset that was inside. "Yes, dear?"

"Will you come up, Mother? Mr. Hamilton's taken a drop too much."

"Yes, dear, of course. I won't be a minute."

She replaced the receiver, and before closing the cupboard rooted around inside it for something, eventually bringing out some knitting and a cooking timer. "Come on, boy."

At the rear of the kitchen there was a door at the top of a flight of steps, leading down to the cellars. In former times they had been dungeons and store-rooms, vaulted chambers hacked out of the living rock and so numerous and extensive that even Willie hadn't fully explored the system. He had managed to wire up several of the chambers, but the few naked electric light bulbs only served to accentuate the shadows.

The noise of their footsteps echoed through the cellars and Willie shivered in delicious anticipation. "Can I fire the torpedoes, Gran?"

"Of course, dear." Mrs. Exe crossed the second chamber and opened the thick oak door to the next one. In the corner of the third dungeon she pressed against one of the stones and a section of the wall rumbled forward. Behind it there was a small recess with a telephone and some switches. On the left-hand wall, at the rear, behind another door, there was a crude, open lift. Willie picked up the telephone.

"All torpedo tubes closed up, sir."

"Right, lad." Hogan's voice was calm. "Send your Granny up, will you."

"Dad wants you to go up, Gran."

Mrs. Exe stepped into the lift, closed the door and began to sort out her knitting as Willie threw one of the switches. "Fire one!" Slowly the lift began to ascend as she concentrated on counting the stitches on her knitting-needles.

In Hamilton's bedroom Hogan heard the click of the arriving lift and pressed the second coloured button. A panel slid aside to reveal his Mother.

"Twenty-seven, twenty-eight, twenty-nine." She looked out at him, beaming. "I thought I'd dropped a stitch, but I haven't." She walked across to the bed and surveyed the snoring man. "He looks very comfortable, dear, doesn't he?"

"Yes, Mother."

She looked round the room with approval. "You know, this *is* a nice room, Hoagy. Did Mr. Hamilton say whether he liked it?"

"He thought it was magnificent."

"Splendid!" She went across to the fireplace and put her knitting and the cooking timer on a small table beside one of the winged armchairs, then plumped herself comfortably in the chair and set the timer. She smiled gently at her waiting son. "All right, you can carry on, dear."

"Yes, Mother." Exe went back to the telephone. "Go ahead, Willie."

In the cellar Willie saluted. "Aye, aye, Captain." He threw the second switch. "All torpedoes fired, sir!"

Exe looked across at the bed. Slowly, silently and inexorably, the padded top of the four-poster began to descend on to the snoring figure below. A massive screwed shaft emerging from the ceiling to push the top down in the manner of a giant press. "Torpedoes running true, Willie."

The lift began to sink from sight and Hogan strolled across to an armchair and sat down, sparing one glance at the bed-top which was now only an inch or so above the unconscious man. Then the recumbent figure was lost to view and Hogan turned his attention to his manicure, taking a nail-file from his pocket and using it diligently while he waited.

There was no sound from the suffocating man; the room was quiet except for the clicking of Mrs. Exe's knitting-needles and the rapid ticking of the cooking timer.

"I think we'd better use up that old meat in the soup tomorrow, Hoagy."

"Just as you say, Mother."

"You must get Willie to build a bigger fridge."

"Tell him what you want and he'll see to it."

She put down her knitting and faced him. "I'll be wanting some more wool before long."

"Willie can get you some while he's away."

"So long as he doesn't go to the place he went to last time. They charge an extra halfpenny an ounce! Sheer robbery. If I had my way people like that would be prose-cuted." The timer gave a startlingly loud *ping*, and she looked at him with satisfaction.

"He's done, dear."

Hogan got to his feet and went to the telephone. "O.K., Willie."

Willie, in the cellar, beamed. "Up periscope! " He dis-engaged one of the switches and in the room two floors above, the head of the four-poster began to rise. Willie stepped into the lift. "Surface, Mister Lieutenant! Blow all tanks! "

Mrs. Exe struggled to her feet and went across to the bed, regarding its occupant benevolently. "He looks very peaceful, Hoagy." She put her head on one side. "Quite a bit of meat on his bones," she added approvingly.

Hogan was brisk now. He congratulated Willie as his son came into view in the rising lift. "Very nice operation, lad. Smooth as silk."

The youth forgot his naval pretence for a moment. "It worked all right, Dad?"

"Doesn't it always! You're a good lad, Willie." He rubbed his hands together. "Well now, everyone. Work to be done! "

With the smoothness of action that comes from practice they manhandled the body from the bed into the lift while Mrs. Exe busied herself removing the dead man's clothing from the wardrobe, throwing it on the bed he had only just involuntarily vacated, then going into the bathroom for his toilet articles.

The two male Exes propped the body in a sitting position in the lift and sent it on its journey to the dungeon below. That done, Exe went to the door, opened it and took a swift peep up and down the corridor. It was deserted and he beckoned Willie out. Togther they strode down the staircase, Willie carefully keeping step, along to the kitchen and down again.

The body was waiting for them and they picked it up, keeping Hamilton upright between them as they entered a passage that led to another dungeon. Willie stretched out his free hand to switch on the lights as they passed through this last doorway, and illuminated a chamber that was rather smaller than the others. But this one wasn't empty.

In the middle of it there was a low deal table and beyond the table a raised ramp carrying a conveyor belt, the end of which passed through a hole in one wall and out of sight. To one side of the underground room there was a pile of heavy rocks and beside these a stack of what looked like wire cages, each about six feet long, two feet wide and two feet deep, standing under some shelving.

The top of the table was covered with a sheet of polythene that draped over the edges and to the granite floor. On the polythene one of the wire cages rested, its lid open, and Hamilton's body was hoisted into it, Willie arranging the limbs decently.

Willie put a couple of the rocks into the cage, then looked at them dubiously. "Shall I put another one in, Dad? He might float. He's pretty big."

"Good idea."

Mrs. Exe entered, a "Thermos" and two cups in her hands. "Everything going well? . . . Splendid, splendid." She held out the cups. "Would you like a drop of soup, Hoagy? It's getting chilly outside and it'll keep the cold out."

"Thank you Mother." He took a sip when she handed him a cup. "I say, this is jolly good! "

"It's a drop of special, love." She beamed at him affectionately. "Put your scarf on when you go out, there's a good boy." She poured some soup for Willie, who had closed the top of the wire cage and was busy pulling the polythene round the whole thing and zipping it closed.

"He's ready, Dad."

"Right, boy." Hogan put down his cup and went to help his son. Together they lifted the plastic-wrapped corpse on to the conveyor belt, Mrs. Exe watching them anxiously.

"Be careful, dears, he's very heavy." She shook her head doubtfully. "I shouldn't go for heavy ones in the future, Hoagy. You might strain yourself."

"We can manage, Gran," Willie said reassuringly. "You ready, Dad?"

"Yes."

"O.K." He drew himself upright and intoned in a solemn voice: "I name this ship the S.S. *Trout's Dinner*." He pressed a button and the conveyor began to move, carrying the encased body of Hugh Hamilton slowly towards the hole in the wall. It disappeared from sight and they listened intently. A few moments later they heard a muffled splash and relaxed.

"Well, I'll be off." Hogan moved to the doorway. "Don't wait up for me, Mother."

"Very well, dear. You won't forget your scarf, will you?

You know your throat's not too strong."

She followed her son, who was taking a different route through the warren of dungeons and passages. In one of the cellars a cadaverous, middle-aged man was seated behind what looked like a large, flat-topped desk, reading a book. As they came into view he looked up at them without speaking. Mrs. Exe smiled across at him. "Good evening, Mr. White. Isn't it good weather!" The thin man watched them out of sight, then turned back to his book.

Hogan climbed a flight of stone steps, used a peephole in a panel at the top and, satisfied, slid the secret door aside, emerging into the empty entrance-hall and closing the panel behind his Mother. From one of the clothes pegs on the wall behind the reception desk he took a scarf, wrapping it round his neck.

"That's a good boy." She nodded approvingly, watching him walk to the entrance.

When Exe stepped out of the front entrance of the castle he stood for a minute, getting his eyes accustomed to the darkness and listening for any sound. But Tam Bruce wasn't about tonight and Hogan stole off silently to where the rowing-boat was tied up.

It was a cloudy night without mist, but although the moon was hidden from view it gave sufficient light for him to see the marker he was looking for. There was a rope tied to the wood float, at the other end of which Hamilton's cage was attached, the plastic envelope giving enough buoyancy to keep the cage a few inches below the surface. With the rope tied to the stern of the boat, Hogan got out the oars and began to row.

His navigation was precise. Only once did he have to look over his shoulder to check his position. When he shipped his oars he loosened the scarf round his throat. His Mother was inclined to fuss a little at times. Then he took out his knife, flicked it open and reached down with it into the water.

Thirty seconds later the rock-weighted wire cage slid deeper, freed from the cut polythene envelope and carrying Hamilton's body downwards. Hogan pulled the split plastic into the boat, put out the oars and began to pull towards the castle, humming tunelessly.

Chapter Four

TAM BRUCE was cycling home from another unproductive foray against the poachers whom he knew infested the area. The sergeant at Mallock was an obstinate, obdurate man who claimed that there was little or no poaching in Tam's district. But Tam knew better, and one fine day he was going to make the seargeant look daft! Aye, he would that!

But for the time being—he turned his head as he became aware of the sound of music. A silver-grey Bentley convertible, with its top down, was movng up behind him. It was being driven by a dark, curly-haired man, about forty, in a short-sleeved pink-striped shirt that showed off his powerful arms and shoulders. The music stopped as the man switched off the car radio and braked to a halt. Tam got off his bicycle.

"Good afternoon, officer."

"Guid afternoon, sir." The mannie was a foreign foreigner. Not one of these foreigners from below the Scottish border, but a foreign foreigner from over the seas, a Yank, from the sound of him.

"I wonder if you can help me? I'm looking for a hotel, an inn—anywhere I can stay."

Tam brightened. "Well, sir, you've asked the man that can tell ye."

He gave detailed instructions as to how to reach Aarolie Castle. "Tell Master Exe I sent you." The American must be very rich to be able to drive such a motor-car; perhaps Exe would consider pouring out an extra dram for such a catch.

Jay Donaldson waved his thanks to the officer as he set

the Bentley in motion. The country was magnificent, the colours even more glorious than he had expected; the tales his grandfather had related, years ago, about the Old Country, as he'd called it, hadn't after all been exaggerated, not as far as the beauty of the landscape was concerned, anyway.

Ten minutes later the Bentley streaked across the open stretch in front of the castle and pulled up with a scrunch of gravel. Selina, who was just crossing the hall, went to the door, then seeing it was a newcomer, walked out hesitantly to greet him. "Good afternoon, sir. Can I help you?" She had to look up at him as he climbed out of the driving seat. He was a big man, almost as large as her uncle, but with a clean-shaven, smiling face. His grin was friendly.

"You've got a room?"

"Yes, sir. For how long?"

He had been about to say he wanted it for one night, but changed his mind. The girl attracted him; he'd been aware of a sharp feeling of pleasure at sight of her; and her voice, with a soft accent that he couldn't quite place, was appealing.

"Two or three nights, I guess."

He turned to look at the sign overhead, shading his eyes against the brightness of the sky. "That's a good advertisement." He laughed. "Do you keep many fish like that around here?"

"The fishing's very good, sir." He was opening the boot now and it was filled with luggage. "There's no one here at the moment to carry your bags, sir, but if you leave what you don't want immediately, it'll be taken up to your room as soon as Mr. Exe returns."

"Mr. Exe? I met a cycling policeman who told me that name. He owns the place?"

"Yes."

"Well, I don't think we need trouble the boss." He lifted

40

the two largest cases from the boot, the muscles of his bare, tanned arms rippling smoothly. "Lead on." She went in front of him, giving him a chance to appraise her figure. In spite of the working clothes she was wearing she was a beauty.

The entrance-hall inspired him to give a quiet whistle of appreciation. This was the real thing, the authentic Scottish atmosphere. He'd been in the place only a moment or two but already he felt—what was the feeling? That he'd like to end his days here, or somewhere exactly like it.

He signed the Registration Book, watched by the girl. "There." He turned the book round and pushed it towards her. "Now you know my name, but I don't know yours."

"Selina, sir." Selina. Unusual and pretty. It suited her. "Miss? Mrs.? and Selina what?"

"Just Selina, sir." Her voice was cold and he could have kicked himself for making such a fatuous approach. What was the matter with him? In the last five years he'd hardly even glanced at a woman yet here he was, making a sort of pass at a girl he hadn't known existed a few minutes earlier. And of course he would go and choose the castle-owner's daughter!

He grinned. "Sorry! I'm not trying to get fresh!"

"That'll be a change." She walked towards the staircase, apparently dismissing the whole tiny incident from her mind. "If you'll come this way, sir."

Suitably chastened, he followed her up the stairs, more interested in her shapely legs than where he was going. At the head of the stairs she turned right and led him to the room that had been occupied up to the previous day by the late Hugh Hamilton.

"Tea will be served in half an hour, sir."

Before he could think of anything to say to keep her she had gone, closing the door behind her silently. Jay put the cases down and stretched himself, looking round the room. It was more or less what he'd expected, but—— He darted to the door and flung it open.

"Hey!"

She was almost at the corner of the corridor, but she stopped and turned to look back inquiringly. "Where's the bathroom?"

"Turn right and it's the first door on the right." She swore mildly under her breath. That was one of the things she should have remembered to tell him.

"Thanks." Jay went back into his room and stretched again, loosening his muscles, then he tried the taps. The cold-water one worked well, but only a trickle came from the other. He shrugged. You couldn't have everything, and the view from the window was a great compensation. "Selina," he said, experimentally. "Sel-ee-*na*." Was she the only daughter of the unknown Mr. Exe, or were there other beautiful young women around?

As he began to unpack he whistled a happy tune. He was going to enjoy life at Aarolie Castle.

"Come in, come in." Selina wondered what Mrs. Exe would be doing this time as she walked into her room. The walls were fitted with wardrobes, their doors open to display the period costumes that crammed all the available space. The old woman was working an antiquated sewing machine, repairing a voluminous dress of the Victorian era. A quarter of a century earlier Mrs. Exe had worked for a theatrical costumier. After some years she had left—taking the stock with her as she could not bear to part with it, but neglecting to pay for it.

"Ah, my dear, what is it?"

"I've just signed a guest in, Aunty. An American."

"An American, eh? Splendid! Everyone knows all Americans are millionaires. . . . What's he like? Old?"

"No. . . . He's rather good-looking."

Mrs. Exe stopped treadling and pulled her glasses down

her nose to peer at the girl. "Good-looking, is he? How refreshing! Still, if he's American . . . ! " She pursed her lips and shook her head in disapproval. "They're not nice people, you know. . . . Remember that." She turned back to her machine and started it working again, apparently forgetting her visitor.

For a moment Selina watched her, then smiled gently and went to her own room. It was large but sparsely furnished. The large wardrobe here was in contrast with those in Mrs. Exe's room, for it was almost empty. Selina made a quick change, taking off the dress she was wearing and donning a waitress's uniform before she went down to get ready to serve teas. For a moment she stood in front of the mirror, smoothing the worn black dress against her body, contemplating the reflection of her figure.

Then she pulled a face at herself and grinned impishly.

"Eejit! "

Hogan Exe was waiting at the station, sitting in the estate car in the yard as the train puffed in. A minute later he saw Willie as the youth climbed out on to the platform and walked along to hand in his ticket. He had the door open as Willie drew near.

"Well?"

"No trouble at all, Dad."

"Did you do as I said?"

"Of course. It was a pity, though." Willie looked mournful. "I could have done with that engine, Dad. It was smashing. I could have run the emergency generator with it."

"I've told you before, boy, we've got to be careful. Organized." He steered out of the yard. "Suppose Tam Bruce came snooping, looking for Hamilton?"

Willie guffawed. "He wouldn't find him."

"Of course not. But suppose he found the engine—found

43

the engine with a number on it that showed it belonged to Hamilton? What then, son?"

The youth shuffled in his seat uncomfortably. "It's an awful waste, Dad."

"I know." Hogan gave it some consideration. "Tell you what. The next car we get we'll sell. You can take it down to Glasgow and get rid of it to that man you know there, that crook who bought the last one from you."

"Promise, Dad?"

"Promise." He looked sideways at his son. "Right. Tell me exactly what you did to-day."

"I did what you told me."

"Good. Now tell me what you did." One had to be patient with Willie at times; he was a good lad but not too bright in some respects, although in others he was almost a genius, and when he finished the space ship he was building, maybe the whole world would recognize the brilliance of Hogan Exe's son.

"I drove the car to Renniton and took it up on the moor."

"And left it there?"

"Yes."

"With the luggage inside?"

"Yes."

"That's a good boy."

The moors at that place were wild, deserted and treacherous. Only last summer the skeletons of two hikers had been found, after they had been missing for three years. When the car was discovered—and that might not take place for weeks—it would be assumed that Hamilton was lost on the moor. Renniton was forty miles south of the place where Hamilton had drawn the money. When the police commenced inquiries it would look as though the missing man had started back towards England after getting the cash from the bank. Certainly there would be nothing to link Aarolie Castle with the mystery; it was eighty miles from there to the spot where the car would be found.

Hogan drove homewards, humming happily to himself.

When they emerged from the belt of trees and Willie saw the silver-grey Bentley, his eyes opened wide. "Golly whumpers! Look at that, Dad!"

But his father was already appraising the expensive car. "It looks brand new."

Willie was out of the estate car and peering excitedly at the dashboard of the Bentley. "She hasn't done a thousand yet!"

"Come away, Willie." Better find out who owned the thing, before letting the youth touch it. "*Willie!*" He glared at the startled young man. "You heard what I said!"

"Yes, Dad." Reluctantly, Willie closed the off-side door of the convertible. When his father got wild it was prudent to obey.

"Go and find your Granny."

Hogan went into the entrance-hall and examined the Registration Book. There was one new entry. Jay Donaldson, an American from some town in the States that Exe had never heard of, was probably the owner of the vehicle. Hogan felt a pulse start to beat in his temple. It wasn't fair that any man in the world should have enough wealth, private wealth, to be able to purchase such a luxury.

Jay Donaldson.

No other signature, so the man must be alone. And Exe had certainly never heard the name before; Donaldson hadn't been to Aarolie before and he hadn't booked a room by post. So it seemed as though the American was a chance guest.

"Gran's in the kitchen, Dad."

"All right, boy."

Exe strolled to the glass-panelled door of the dining-room. Four men were taking tea and one of them was a stranger. Hogan studied the man. He was in his late thirties, with a handsome, sunburned face and dark curly hair. The

45

hotel proprietor shook his head regretfully. Such a man would almost certainly be married. As like as not he'd be telephoning the United States every other night to speak to his wife—unless she was on her way to join him. Or maybe she was shopping in London.

Selina had gone up to the stranger to see if he had all he needed. He was smiling and shaking his head and Exe chose that moment to enter the room. He walked straight over to Donaldson's table.

"Good afternoon, sir. Everything all right? My name's Exe. Is my niece looking after you well?"

Jay looked up at the towering, bearded figure. "Yes, thanks." So the girl was a niece, not his daughter. "You've got a magnificent setting here, Mr. Exe."

"Yes." He paused. "You'll be here for the fishing?"

"Partly."

"I see." Exe didn't ask the obvious question. "Well, we'll have a chat about that later on, sir." He nodded abruptly, then went out to talk to his mother. One of his black moods was coming on and he'd better tell her. She was putting a casserole on to a tray when he reached the kitchen. He looked at her significantly and she nodded. "Just a little something to keep the wolves away, Hoagy."

He ran his fingers through his beard. "I want to talk, Mother."

"Then why don't you go to see you-know-who?"

"Maybe I'll do that. But first I'll go to my room."

She smiled understandingly. "There's a full bottle in there. I'll see that you're not disturbed, my son." He strode off and she watched him go, then, turning back to pick up the tray, she gave a piercing shriek as she saw Selina standing beside her. "*Selina!*" She pressed a hand against her bosom. "You frightened me half to death!"

"I've finished the teas, Aunty."

"That's a good girl." Mrs. Exe looked round vaguely, for inspiration. "I'm just going to have a little rest before dinner," she said at last. "I think we could do with a few more peeled carrots."

"I'll start on them now." Peeling vegetables was the job Selina hated most of all the chores she had to do. Although there were only ever a few guests at a time at the castle, with only four of them to do the work she had to be on the job sixteen hours a day.

As she went to the vegetable store, Selina saw Mrs. Exe start off furtively with a tray of food. It was the regular routine and Selina didn't know whether to be amused or worried about it.

Hogan had just finished his second drink of neat whisky, pacing up and down the bedroom as the pressures inside his skull seemed to build up intolerably. His black moods were becoming more frequent lately, and oddly enough they occurred after he had committed a smart piece of business. Hugh Hamilton, for example. He had been a stroke of good fortune.

He went to the window, drawing in deep breaths of the tangy, pine-scented air. As he did so he saw a flicker of movement among the undergrowth beside the edge of the loch. Was it Tam Bruce lurking there, hoping to catch his poachers? Through his binoculars, Exe discovered the identity of the walker. It was Jay Donaldson.

Thoughtfully, Hogan put down the binoculars. Was the American very rich? He must be well-off to be able to run a Bentley—unless it was hired? Of course, an American would be a great risk—there'd be the devil of a hue and cry after a missing Yankee. But if Donaldson were a suitable candidate for club membership . . . ?

Thinking about business had made him feel better. He took the glasses again and, after a minute's search, spotted the American again. Although because of the lie of the land in relation to the water, Donaldson wasn't more than a quarter of a mile distant, it would take him at least a full mile's walk to get back to the castle, and the ground was rough and broken. So, the man couldn't get back in less than a quarter of an hour.

Hogan's mood swung to one of elation. He wanted to talk to someone, but first he'd take the opportunity that offered itself and look round Donaldson's room, on the floor below. It wouldn't take him long to do so.

The quick search was instructive. Donaldson's clothes were expensive, his fishing tackle the finest. There was a telescopic rifle in a leather case and a pair of Purdey shotguns, but he spared them only a glance. What he was looking for were personal items, letters, documents.

"Ah!"

In one of the bottom drawers of the chest there was a large, thick-leaved album, hidden away under a pile of clean shirts. As he drew it out he saw the gold lettering on the black leather cover: *PERSONAL CUTTINGS: Jay Donaldson*.

"A blasted actor!"

But when he opened the book and leafed through the pages he saw he had been wrong, and the headlines of one of the pasted-in newspaper cuttings made his eyes open wide: LOCAL BOY HAS IT MADE . . . DONALDSON'S ELECTRONICS SOLD FOR THREE MILLION DOLLARS. 'J.D.' RETIRES AT 39.

There must have been a hundred cuttings, all relating to the sale of the manufacturing company that Jay Donaldson had built from nothing. Varying likenesses of Donaldson peered out from the printed pages and as Hogan read extracts from some of the columns, his excitement mounted. It looked very much as though the new occupant of this room was a millionaire, even by British standards.

Which made him eminently suitable for the Club, assuming there were no snags.

In the bar, after dinner, Jay was delighted to find that

there was little or none of the English reticence he had heard about, at any rate so far as the bearded proprietor of the hotel was concerned. Hogan Exe was in a friendly mood and seemed to be really interested in his guest.

Jay was even more impressed when, with all the other guests retired for the night, he was invited into Hogan's office. He went round the room examining the specimens in glass cases, barely able to believe what he saw. "These are *real*?"

Hogan's lips split in a grin. He was feeling marvellously at the top of his form. "That's what they all say, Mr. Donaldson, first time they see those cases. They're real enough." He settled back in his chair. "The record fish taken from the loch was thirty-seven pounds, two ounces. And that was killed two years back. Mark you, the Scottish record's a bit more than that. Thirty-nine and a half pounds —and that was taken in 1886, so I reckon it'll stand for a bit longer, but we're pushing it, sir, we're pushing it."

Donaldson laughed. "You know, my old grandfather used to tell me yarns when I was a kid, about how he used to get twenty-pounder trout when he was in this country." He shook his head. "I never did believe him, but now, well . . ."

"I've got a theory that there's more than one *fifty*-pounder in the loch," Exe said earnestly.

An hour ago the American would have laughed at such an assertion, but now he'd seen the stuffed monsters in the cases on the walls, he wasn't so sure.

"You won't get them in the streams," Exe continued. "Not big 'uns, because there isn't enough for them to feed on. But in the loch . . . you know trout will eat anything. You've got to feed 'em if there isn't enough natural food. But here . . . You saw how sheer the drop to the water is in places? I think the loch trout feed well because of those sheer drops. Plenty of deer on the mountains and it stands to sense that some of 'em die by falling into the water.

"If there are poachers about, what easier way to get rid of the evidence of a kill than to sling the offal into the loch?" He drained his brandy glass. "All good food for the trout, Mr. Donaldson. They'll take whatever's offered."

Jay's eyes glittered at the thought of hooking a fifty-pound giant. A fish that size on the end of your line would like as not jerk your arms out of their sockets. "You know, I never gave much thought to what they ate. I just took it for granted that they made do with flies."

"Lord, no! Trout are cannibals, even." He roared with laughter. "Why, they'd even make a meal off you if you let 'em!"

"Not much fear of that!" Jay joined in the laughter. "Mind you, if I'd carried on with my business a year or two longer I might have felt like chucking myself in as fish food."

Exe slapped his thigh in an ecstasy of enjoyment. "My word, sir, I like a man with a sense of humour!"

The comment had seemed ordinary enough to Jay and he glanced uncertainly at the other man, wondering what it was that was so funny. "No, I really mean it. You know, I slaved away at that business, really slaved. I ate, breathed, drank and slept Donaldson's Electronics Incorporated. I thought I was building a road—a road to freedom, but I found I was making a cage for myself. A cage that got smaller and smaller, restricting me more and more every day, until it looked as though the cage was going to turn into a coffin."

He was too involved in his own story to notice the expression on the listener's face. "I suddenly realized where I was heading and I had to get away! I had to get rid of it all, enjoy myself while I was young enough to do just that! If I'd have stuck it another ten years I'd have been an old man, not a middle-aged guy. An old man. I wanted freedom and peace."

Hogan was nodding sympathetically. "I know exactly

how you feel, sir. Exactly. And if I may say so, I think you've come to the right place to find what you're looking for. Give it a week or two, sir, and I think I can guarantee you won't have a care on your mind and that you'll have all the peace any man can hope for on this earth.''

Chapter Five

IT was getting on for midnight when Selina finished the washing-up and went into the hotel dining-room to lay the tables for breakfast. She switched two of the lights on and was changing the tablecloths when she heard the door from the entrance-hall creak open behind her. Startled she looked round.

"Hi!"

It was the American and at the sight of his smiling face she gave a sigh of relief. His smile changed to a look of concern. "Did I startle you?"

"I—I thought it was someone else."

He considered the statement. She'd looked frightened. Of whom? Was one of the guests being a nuisance? "I was going out to take a breath of air before going to bed." He moved nearer. "You're working late. Let me help you."

"No, thank you, sir. I always do this."

"Always? Don't you take time off?"

She didn't answer and he accepted defeat. Perhaps it wasn't the best time of day—or night—to work on getting acquainted. "Well, I'll be on my way. Good night, Selina."

"Good night, sir."

When he had gone she remained for a few seconds, staring after him, her blue eyes wistful, then with a sigh she went on with the work to be done. It was almost finished. Only the clean napkins had to be put out now. She went to the tall, built-in cupboard and stretched up to reach for the napkins where they were kept on a shelf above eye-level.

Snap.

With a gasp of shock and pain she snatched her hand

away. Dangling from the first three fingers of her right hand was a mousetrap.

"*Willie!* You rotten little . . . ! " She struggled to release the trap and dropped it on the floor, nursing her stinging fingers and blowing on them to ease the pain. After a few moments her fright was gone and she was more angry than anything else. She picked up the mousetrap, putting it in the pocket of her overall. "You won't do that a third time, young Willie! " She put the napkins out and switched off the lights.

Upstairs she hurried along the corridor, pulling the mousetrap from her pocket and putting out a hand to grasp the knob of a closed door. Then she thought better of it and went towards a flight of narrow, spiral stairs, which she mounted.

Willie, crouched, listening at his door, and as her footsteps moved on he grinned, hugging himself with pleasure. He performed a crazy little jig, then drew himself up to attention and saluted.

"Anything on the hydrophones, Bosun?"

"On listening watch, sir."

A long, flat-topped cupboard ran the length of one wall. It was covered with bits of radio and engineering equipment, including a stripped-down gear-box. In the angle of the two walls on the other side of the room there was a double-tiered ship's bunk which acted as a bed on the top layer and a repository for more pieces of equipment on the lower one.

Donning a worn uniform hat that had once belonged to a naval officer, Willie clambered up on to the top bunk and settled himself, cap still on his head. Beside his right hand, mounted on a panel, were the knobs, dials and loudspeaker grille of a radio set. He turned a knob and the set clicked into life, then tuned one of the dials accurately.

Above his head there was a complicated mass of levers and wheels that had, at its lowest point, an eyepiece.

"Up periscope, Mr. Mate."

"Aye, aye, sir."

He reached up to grip the handles on either side of the eyepiece, bringing the glass down until he could peep into it, then began to turn one of the wheels. Outside the window a narrow tube began to extend upwards.

For a time there was nothing in the eyepiece, then he grinned as it showed a light. He manœuvred the wheels and levers with the familiarity of experience until he had a view of the bedroom immediately above—Selina's—the homemade periscope peering in through the gap left over the top of the drawn curtains.

Selina was smoothing something on to the backs of the first three fingers of her right hand and Willie crowed with delight.

"Number One torpedo hit, sir!"

He watched with eager anticipation for her to go into the regular routine she employed every night. She'd take off her overall, then remove her dress and put on her dressing-gown so that she could sit in front of the mirror brushing her hair. And when she'd done that she'd open the second drawer where she kept her underclothes and take out the ones she was going to wear next day.

When she opened the drawer tonight . . . He giggled.

Selina's movements were slower than usual. As she prepared for bed she was thinking of the American, listening in memory to the soft depth of his voice and the sympathy in his tone. *"Let me help you."*

She shook back her blonde hair and looked sternly at her reflection in the glass. "What's the use of dreaming!" She moved briskly now, completing the last few brush strokes. She put down the brush and reached out to open the drawer in which she kept her underclothing. As she pulled the drawer open she screamed in terror. Something monstrous sprang from it, almost hitting her in the face then swaying backwards and forwards in front of her.

Out on the lochside Jay Donaldson heard the thin echoes of the scream and looked back over his shoulder, frowning uncertainly at the huge black mass of Aarolie Castle, just visible in the darkness. Had it been a human scream? "Maybe some animal," he reassured himself.

Selina was staring in sick dismay at the thing that had frightened her. It was something like a huge jack-in-the-box, the long swaying stalk of a cloth-covered spring topped by a half-size model of a human skull. She snatched the obscene thing from the drawer, ripping it free from the underclothes and throwing it wildly across the floor.

"Beast! Beast!"

Sobbing, she flung herself on to the bed and pressed her weeping face into the pillow, beating a clenched fist against it in impotent rage.

Mrs. Exe was reading *The Vampires of Doom* comfortably in bed when someone tapped on the door. She put the luridly-covered book down. "Come in, dear." It could only be her son, at this hour. Hogan walked over to the bed. She peered up at him over the top of her round spectacles and nodded in approval. "You've had a nice long talk." She was at her most maternal-looking, her lace-trimmed nightcap framing a gently-smiling face.

"Yes." He pulled out a chair and straddled it, facing her. "I've had two talks. The first one was with the American."

"Mr. Donaldson? . . . Selina thinks he's good-looking, although I prefer men with a bit more meat on them."

"Donaldson's got some meat in his bank account, I shouldn't wonder."

She peered across at him. "Is he suitable?"

"I don't know—yet. We've got to play this one carefully, Mother. He could be a record catch." He paused. "I'm taking him across the loch in the morning."

Mrs. Exe reached out a hand to pat her son's knee. "I'll see what I can find, dear." She took a box of chocolates from her bedside table. "Would you like a peppermint cream?" He shook his head and she selected one, popping it into her mouth. "If business is going to increase, Hoagy, I shall want more wire."

"I'll see to it."

"Thank you, darling." She held up her cheek to be kissed. "Sleep well, son."

"Good night, Mother."

"God bless, son! " He closed the door softly behind him and she picked up the paperback, settling down to it with fresh gusto.

Jay ran down the magnificent staircase and breezed into the dining-room. He nodded to the other men present; they were at the toast and marmalade stage. Hogan, dressed ready for outdoors, waited on him. "I thought I was early, Mr. Exe, but that Highland air . . . ! "

Hogan nodded. "It's a great place for sleeping well, sir. . . . A great place."

The American wanted to put a question about the girl, but thought better of it. She'd been working late the previous evening; maybe this was her day off? He grinned up at the bearded man, who was clearing the first course away. "I haven't forgotten what you said last night, Mr. Exe. You personally guaranteed me a monster."

"I'll do my best."

The man was so quietly confident that there didn't seem anything more to say.

The moment he had finished his meal, Jay went to get his fishing gear. He carried it down and outside to find Exe waiting at the point where the rowing-boat was tied up. The morning was grey, with heavy clouds obscuring the whole of the sky, the still water of the loch reflecting the greyness.

"Is it going to rain?"

Exe shook his head. "I don't think so." He held the boat

steady while Jay climbed aboard, then got in himself and took the oars. He pulled the boat through the water at surprising speed, not appearing to feel any strain. They were half-way across before either of them spoke, and it was Jay who broke the silence.

"Would you mind if I rowed? It's been some time since I handled a pair of oars."

Exe looked concerned. "It's dangerous to change seats in a boat, Mr. Donaldson. One of us—you—might fall in." He smiled. "I don't want to lose you."

"That's all right. I can swim."

"Very well, sir, if you insist."

From an upstairs window of the castle Mrs. Exe was watching the boat and its passengers through binoculars. She frowned as she saw the manœuvre going on. The American edged forward to the centre, holding on to Exe as they changed places. Jay's foot slipped, making the boat lurch and nearly throwing him over the side. Only the fact that Exe was holding one of his arms saved Jay from falling backwards into the water.

Mrs. Exe gasped. "Be careful, dear!"

The hotel proprietor's grip was like a steel band; he had the strenth of three men. Jay rubbed the spot where he had been grasped. "Thanks. You saved me from becoming a trout's lunch."

For a moment Hogan looked startled, then his teeth gleamed in the darkness of his beard. "It's all part of the service."

Jay had the oars now and the boat began to move, but not nearly so fast as before. He smiled at Exe. "Guess I'm not so good at it as you."

"I'm used to the boat."

Within five minutes Jay was sorry he had asked to row. It was humiliating to know that the other man, ten or fifteen years older, was the fitter of the two. "I'm out of condition, I guess."

"Give you a few days here, Mr. Donaldson, and you'll be in prime condition. I guarantee it."

"Like you guaranteed the monster?"

"Exactly."

"I'll take you up on that."

"Please do."

Mrs. Exe bolted the door of Donaldson's room and began a leisurely search. The cuttings book was where Hogan had said it was and she leafed through its pages calmly, looking up once or twice to make sure the boat was not returning.

One newspaper clipping made her stop. "A genius! So the boy's a genius."

The headline was in tall enough type to be seen from the other side of the room. FORMER BOY GENIUS BECOMES MULTI-MILLIONAIRE. She adjusted her glasses in order to read the smaller type, then turned to look out of the window. The boat was out of sight now. "Take care of the dear boy, Hoagy. Take care of him."

Some of Jay's enthusiasm had left him. After several hours' fishing the result was one broken line and a lost hook. Was it his own fault? All the trout-fishing he had ever done before had been in streams, where it was comparatively easy to spot the likely places to fish. But in the still waters of Loch Aarolie it wasn't so simple.

If there'd been any rises along the stretch he'd fished, he hadn't seen them. So far he'd taken Exe's advice, but now it was beginning to look as though the bearded giant was playing him for a sucker. Exe hadn't spoken for hours. He'd produced the cold lunch and was now sitting back taking his ease.

Jay examined the dry-fly he was using and wondered whether to bother casting again. He was just about to turn and speak to Exe when the big man moved silently behind

him, gripping his arm and pointing. Then Jay saw it. A fish
was rising, leaving a widening ripple on the surface of the
water. There was another rise, then another. With the next
one, Jay made up his mind. He cast so that the fly settled
ahead of the line of rises and seconds later he knew he had
a fish on.

Hogan gripped his wrist. "Slowly! "

"O.K." Despite his urge to strike immediately, he did as
he was told and allowed the fish another split-second before
he struck. In fishing a stream he would have struck at once,
but Exe had said that still-water trout needed a bit of time
to take the lure.

"Oh, boy! " The youthful exuberance was forced from
him as he felt the pull on the line. The hooked fish was going to give him a mighty struggle before he got it ashore.
The strength of the creature was enormous; it was almost
like trying to keep a small submarine from getting away, but
no sub could possibly move and change direction with that
speed.

The fight went on for what seemed ages and at one dreadful moment he thought he'd lost the beast. But it was all
right, the fish was tiring and when it broke surface he felt
a fresh thrill. It was a big one without a doubt.

The second it was safe he eased his grip on the rod. His
arms had been aching from the strain of rowing and this
new tension made his hands tremble.

"Congratulations, sir! " Exe was looking up at him from
where he crouched over a fish-scale, the dead fish lying
limp in the pan. "Thirteen pounds, five ounces." He stood
up. "Not a *real* monster, but a good start."

Jay stared at the fish in wonder. "I've never taken a trout
a quarter that size! "

Hogan held the fish at arm's length. "It's not too bad.
But you'll do better than that, sir, you'll do better than that.
You just mark my words! "

"I hope I shall, Mr. Exe." He moved his elbows in

circles, easing the soreness in his shoulders and arms. "But not to-day."

Selina was behind the bar when Jay went for a drink before dinner. Three of the four stools at the bar were occupied by other guests and one of them raised a hand in welcome. "Did you have a good day?"

"Good enough for a start." He perched himself on the vacant stool and smiled at the girl. "Scotch and water, please."

When she placed the glass in front of him he noticed the line of bruising across the first three fingers. "How did you do that?"

"I—I just knocked myself." The question seemed as though it embarrassed her. She snatched her hand away and turned to avoid speaking to him. He found himself staring at her lovely profile, wondering what he had done wrong. She was looking up at the small clock above the bar.

"Dinner'll be served in ten minutes, gentlemen. If you want another drink . . .?" No one did and she left the bar, holding herself stiffly erect.

"Nice piece of goods, eh?"

Donaldson jerked his head to stare at the speaker, a stout, elderly man named Giddon, sitting next to him. Giddon smiled tolerantly; it hadn't needed a sixth sense to guess the American's thoughts as he watched Selina leave.

"She's a pretty girl."

"Yes." Jay wondered just how obvious he had made himself. "Yes, she's lovely," he said coolly. Was Giddon the man who was pestering her?

Giddon dismissed any more reference to the girl and got down to serious talk. "Did you have a good catch?"

"Not bad, not bad at all." He permitted himself an exaggeration. "The biggest one was about thirteen and a half pounds." Giddon was probably used to the waters and to admit to just one fish would brand Jay as an amateur.

The older man sighed. "Wish I could afford to catch one of those brutes."

"I thought you were here for the fishing?" Jay asked, surprised.

"Yes, I am. But I can't afford to go for the monsters."

"I—I don't understand?"

"You have to pay through the nose to be given the chance of killing something big," Giddon explained. "Not that I'm complaining. I always hope that some day one of those monsters will stray to the bit of water where I"—he gestured to include the other two men—"where we fish."

There was something here that Donaldson didn't quite follow. Exe hadn't mentioned anything about additional charges. "You've stayed here before?"

"I've come up here every season for the past six years. Found it by accident. Chap named Renflow—he's dead now, poor devil—we booked in at another place and there was a mix-up over rooms. So they sent us on here—the castle had just been opened as an hotel."

"And I've come up here every year since." He chuckled. "Mind you, although I don't get a crack at the monsters, the sport here's better than anywhere else I've ever known." He regarded the American with amused eyes. "I wonder if you'll be given the ceremony?"

"Ceremony?"

"They serve the fish you caught." The mention of this seemed to fill him with glee and he burst into almost uncontrollable laughter, his large frame shaking on the small bar stool. At last he gasped, wiping his eyes. "Once or twice a year they put on the ceremony. You're *really* honoured if they do that."

Jay had an uneasy feeling that his leg was being pulled. But beyond that there was a growing resentment. Was Exe taking him for a ride—going to charge him double for every item? But the stout man was speaking again, breathless from his bout of laughter.

"They're a rum bunch, wouldn't you say—excepting the girl, of course."

"Rum?"

"Between you and me, friend," Giddon lowered his voice, "at least one of 'em should be in the looney bin . . . That Willie?"

"Willie?"

"Haven't you had the pleasure of meeting young Master Exe? It's a joy in store for you if you haven't."

"You mean Hogan's son?"

"That's the boy. Keen on practical jokes, you know. And *that's* a sign of arrested development." He edged himself off the stool. "Don't take too much notice of me, lad. I think I'm jealous of your catch . . . if you know what I mean."

Donaldson didn't. It seemed to him that the old man himself was a bit round the bend. But then the bell that announced dinner sounded and he was suddenly conscious of being very, very hungry. He made his way to the dining-room and was amused to see Giddon intent on his soup, spooning it up at a prodigious rate and not sparing a glance for anyone.

As Selina came up to his table Jay rubbed his hands together briskly. "What have we got?" He took the menu card. "I could eat a horse." A smile lit her face for a moment heightening her beauty. He was suddenly and un-reasonably annoyed with her that she didn't go round smiling most of the time; her presence brightened the austere surroundings.

"I understand from your uncle that I get to eat my own trout. Is that right?"

"It won't taste like horse," she assured him gravely, but then the flash of spirit died and she was back to what was normal for her, cold and reserved, as though she was too scared to relax.

"You'll take the soup, sir?"

"I guess that'll do."

Working in this place couldn't be much fun for her. He looked round at the other guests. There were six of them and they were all years older than himself. It must be dull for any girl, let alone one with looks like Selina's.

He was just finishing his soup when he was startled by a weird noise that after a moment he recognized as bagpipe music. There was no piper present and then he realized the music was coming over a loudspeaker. Five of the other six men were looking expectantly at the green-baize covered doors that led from the kitchen. Only old Giddon paid no attention; bending over a heaped plate, he was stoking away food as though he had not eaten for years.

One of the double doors was pulled open to reveal Exe. The bearded man was dressed in chef's white clothing with a tall, white hat making him appear even more enormous. He held a large silver dish in outstretched arms and began solemnly to march towards the American.

Jay watched, fascinated, as a stout, elderly woman clad in robes that represented Britannia, followed Hogan, smilingly nodding to the male diners. Exe was at Jay's table now and he stood waiting for the woman to reach him. He placed the dish reverently on the table and as he did so the bagpipe wailing stopped abruptly.

"Your trout, sir." Exe's tones were deeper than usual; the words rolled through the dining-room like organ notes.

"It looks great! " Jay was gazing at the fish. Whoever had cooked it had presented it magnificently.

"My Mother cooked it, Mr. Donaldson."

"We hope you like it, my dear."

The soft, slightly breathless voice was motherly. He felt warmed by her regard, although what the costume signified didn't register. Maybe a custom? "I'm sure I shall." He watched Exe, who was in the process of carving a slice from the fish; he placed it on a plate in front of Jay.

"If you would taste this, sir, and see if you approve?"

Jay took a generous portion and put it in his mouth, chewing slowly and savouring the taste. It was hardly necessary to chew really; the flesh almost melted on his tongue and the flavour was ambrosial. He swallowed it, trying to think of a word to describe the sensation. "Wonderful! "

Exe was still hovering. "I hope you'll agree that you've never tasted anything like that before, sir?"

Another mouthful convinced Donaldson. "You're absolutely right! " he confirmed enthusiastically.

"Then may I serve a further portion, sir?"

"You certainly may." He looked up at the woman. "It's sensational."

"There isn't a fish in the world that has the flavour of our loch trout. I'm so glad you like my cooking, Mr. Donaldson. . . . But now I really must get back to my work."

He watched her go, then turned to look at Exe. The big man was wearing the cook's outfit. Surely the old dame hadn't done the cooking dolled up like that? "Did your Mother cook this?"

"Mother cooks everything, sir."

Well, that didn't explain why her son dressed up, but at that moment who the hell cared about such trivial mysteries? Jay took up his knife and fork again as Hogan stepped back. No, it certainly hadn't been an illusion. The taste was still out of this world. "Wonderful," he said again. "Absolutely unique."

Hogan bowed his assent. "If I may say so, sir, it always seems as though there's more *body* in our trout, if you will excuse the expression."

Chapter Six

MRS. EXE peered round the door that led into the entrance-hall and made sure no one was about. The massive front doors were open and the evening sunlight streamed in, but the place was deserted. She scurried across the floor to the post-box, unlocking it with a key she took from her pocket and taking half a dozen letters from it. She went over to the reception desk, sorting over the letters as she did so.

"Ha! "

One of the envelopes was addressed to a town in the United States and this one she put aside. The others she took no exception to; she knew the places to which they were going. Peering round once again to make sure she was alone, she ripped open the letter for America and glanced at the signature.

"We can't have that! "

She stuffed the letter and envelope into one of the desk drawers, then returned the others to the post-box. As she did so, Willie sauntered into view, indulging in a little imaginary overarm bowling.

"You're out! "

Mrs. Exe gave a muffled scream and turned, one hand pressed against her bosom to still the wild fluttering of her heart. "Willie, you naughty boy! You frightened me."

"Did I, Gran?" He grinned with pleasure. "I like scaring people."

"Yes, well, you mustn't scare me, my dear. You know how it upsets me."

"I won't do it again, Gran."

"There's a good boy." She looked round uncertainly. "What time is it?"

From an inner pocket he took a silver hunter, flicking open the lid with an air of importance. "It's nigh on six o'clock, Gran."

"Then I must get on with my work. You stay here, Willie. You know what to do, don't you?"

"See as nobody posts any more letters till the mail van's been."

His grandmother smiled lovingly at him. "That's a good boy."

"But I don't have to do that now, Gran. You watch." He went up to the oaken box that was used to collect the mail and reached one arm round the back. "Look!" He moved his arm and as he did so the slot in the box was closed by a matching piece of wood sliding into the hole from inside the box and filling it. Another movement of his arm and a second slot appeared, higher up.

"If you post anything in that new slot it doesn't fall down into the box, Gran. It stays hidden up top."

Her admiration was unbounded. "My, my! I always said you'd go far, my boy."

"It's clever, isn't it?" He paused, appraising her mood. "As I don't have to stay here, Gran, can I go out?"

"All right, dear, but only for half an hour." She patted his arm approvingly. "Run along now." Suddenly her face went blank. "Dinner! And it's rent day!" Without paying any further attention to the youth she hurried off.

As soon as she had gone Willie produced the silver hunter again and opened its case. "Half an hour." He studied the figures with intense concentration, then rubbed his thumb across the engraved letters on the inside of the front cover:

Hugh Hamilton, Esq.
On the Twenty-fifth Anniversary
of the Founding of Hamilton's
Stores.

THE CATCH

*Presented by Grateful Members
of his Staff.   19.10.46.*

The sound of voices roused him and he hurriedly stuffed
the watch back out of sight into his clothing. Two of the
hotel guests came in at the front door and he ran swooping
past them, mowing them down with an invisible machine-
gun as he passed.

The two men exchanged long-suffering glances, then
looked back after the youth. "Someone should do that to
him."

"Not with an imaginary gun."

Mrs. Exe placed a cloth over the items on the tray and
looked across at Selina, who was tasting something out of
one of the saucepans simmering on the gigantic range. "I'll
just be taking a little breather for a few minutes, dear," she
called to the girl.

Selina turned to look at the old woman, trying to conceal
a smile. "All right, Aunty." She watched Mrs. Exe go pad-
ding off, carrying the tray.

When Mrs. Exe got through the door she turned left,
along the passage that led to the cellars. Slowly she panted
her way down the steps and into the first dungeon, switching on the lights with her elbow as she went. It was a long,
erratic walk to where she wanted to get, but eventually she
arrived at the vast chamber where, on the other side, a man
was sitting behind what looked like a huge desk.

"Din-dins!" she said brightly, as she approached him.
"You're late!"

She placed the tray carefully on the desk, well out of his
reach. "Hasn't it been a beautiful day. All that sunshine. I
declare, it makes you feel good to be alive."

The restraint he had placed upon himself vanished and
he stretched out towards the food. "Please, please," he
begged.

Mrs. Exe regarded him, head tipped to one side. "We

mustn't eat without first washing our hands, now must we." He stared at her, all hope dying. "Go on, be a good boy."

Despairingly he reached up and unlooped a coil of chain that hung above his head. Untied, it fell level with his eyes, an endless set of stout, steel links. Suddenly he stretched his hands and gripped one side of the chain, pulling it down swiftly, then reaching up again to grasp it higher up. As he worked frantically he began slowly to move sideways.

Mrs. Exe nodded approval. The whole apparatus was working smoothly, the steel chair to which he was clamped moved easily on the rails on which it was mounted. Gradually, still pulling with mad speed, he disappeared behind a screen. After a few moments the noise of chains stopped and there was silence, followed by the noise of a water-closet flushing.

There was silence for another few moments then the noise of the chains began again and slowly White came into view, this time pulling on the opposite side of the loop of chain. He reached his former position and stopped, panting.

"Tie the chain up, dear." He did as he was told. "Now show me your hands." He held them out for inspection and she nodded. "There's a clean boy."

He was almost exhausted by his violent exercise with the pulley chain. "Please!" His throat worked agonizingly as he watched her move the cloth covering the tray. But instead of food she brought out something that looked like a cheque-book and a separate piece of paper. She pushed the book over to where he could just reach it. "You haven't forgotten what day it is?"

He put his hands together in an attitude of prayer. "Have pity on me, Mrs. Exe. Have pity, I beg you."

Her voice was very firm, as though dealing with a stubborn, unreasonable child. "Now, Mr. White, we've been over all this before. I'm sure we're looking after you very nicely and if you *will* stay at an hotel, why then you must expect to pay your bill." She held out the sheet of paper. "It's all here, every item. . . . Do you want me to go through them with you?"

There was no more fight left in him. "Give me the pen."

"*Please . . .!*"

"Give me the pen, *please.*"

"That's a good boy." Carefully she edged the fountain-pen just within his reach. He had to strain forward to get his fingertips to it, but at last he managed to pull it towards him, with the book, and sign. That done he pushed them away so that they shot over to her and she stopped them in time from falling to the floor. She examined the signature.

"*Charles White.* . . . Splendid." Taking a plastic bowl from the tray, she put it on the desk-like table, then put a plastic spoon in the stew that half-filled the bowl. Using the tray lengthwise, she pushed the bowl towards him. When it was within reach she pulled the tray back and watched him start to spoon up the food with the desperate urgency of a starving man.

"I've told you again and again," she chided, "not to eat so fast. You'll get indigestion."

The food in the bowl disappeared at an alarming rate and before he pushed it back to her he licked round the edges and ran his finger round the bottom, sucking off what bit of juice he managed to gather. Panting, he stared at her, knowing it was useless to beg for more. "Did you bring me something to read?"

"I gave you something only the other day."

"I've read it. I've read it a dozen times."

"Well, I'm sorry, my dear, but we can't afford to buy books for you all the time. If you'll give me some extra money, I'll buy whatever books you like."

"How can I give you more money? You have every

penny I get."

"Then those who can't afford a thing must learn to do without it, mustn't they!" Her bright smile and air of sweet reasonableness made him want to scream. He'd tried it when they'd first put him down here. . . . How long ago was that? . . . But you could have a regiment of women screaming down here without the sound being heard by anyone above.

She was putting the things back on the tray now and he grew desperate. Bad enough though it was to have her here, it was ten times worse without human company. "Can't you stay and talk?"

"Dear me, no. I've got work to do. Not like you, sitting around all day." She had started to leave when she turned back. "I nearly forgot! Did you like the meat?"

"It—it was all right."

"Good." She smiled, well pleased. "I've been trying another butcher. He's at least a penny a pound cheaper than the one I've had before. Honestly, these butchers! Robbers, that's what they are. Nothing but robbers."

Tam Bruce cycled slowly and majestically across the open ground in front of the castle and dismounted on the terrace near the front entrance. For a moment he stared fiercely into the surrounding mountains as though expecting to see a gang of poachers at work, then, hitching his belt, he went inside.

The entrance-hall was empty and he went through to the little bar, where Exe hailed him from behind the counter. "Come to arrest us all, Tam?"

Bruce considered the question in dignified silence before he answered. "I'm no' here for that, Mr. Exe," he said at last. The braw American mannie was perched on one of the stools. If he, Tam, played his cards right. . . . "Good evening, sir." He touched the brim of his uniform cap with one fingertip.

"Good evening, constable." Jay grinned, knowing precisely what was in the other man's mind. "Give Mr. Bruce whatever he chooses."

"That's verra guid of ye, sir, but I'm on duty. However, if Mr. Exe could put it in a wee bottle, I could have it later, for medicinal purposes."

"You do that, Mr. Bruce." Jay kept his face straight. "You'll be out on crime patrol?"

"Aye. There's an awful lot o' crime in these parts, Mr. Donaldson. An awful lot.'

"I wouldn't have thought it."

"Oh, aye, it isna' yon Chicago that has all the gangsters . . . We have some terribles ones hereabouts. . . . Poachers."

Jay grinned ruefully. The locals were ribbing him. "A dreadful crime," he admitted solemnly.

"Aye. But one of these days I'll lay hands on the culprits, ye can rest assured on that." He took a small bottle from Hogan and slipped it into a rear trouser pocket. "Thank ye kindly, Mr. Donaldson. I'll be saluting your health wi' a sip later on." From his left breast pocket he produced a number of cards and put them on the counter.

"You'll be taking your usual ticket for the Police Dance, Mr. Exe?"

"Of course, Tam."

The tickets had been placed strategically for the American to see and Jay looked down at them. The idea of a dance suddenly appealed to him; he hadn't been to one in years. Would Selina go with him? "I'll take two if I may."

"That'll be twenty-one shillings, sir. You won't regret it, I assure you. It's a grand affair; the laird himself will be there."

"Will there be any other Donaldsons there, do you think?"

Tam regarded the American gravely. "Kinfolk?"

Jay shrugged. "I don't know. My old Grandpa came from these parts though, years back. About 1890 I guess, when he

71

left."

"There was a Donaldson croft up to Craig McMellar," Bruce said thoughtfully. "It's been deserted since before my day."

The American was oddly excited. "Craig McMellar? Where's that?"

"Och, twenty-five, thirty miles to the north-east, but double that distance by road."

"Are there any other Donaldsons in the area?"

Tam shook his head decisively. "No." He checked the time. "I'll be away, gentlemen." He marched out of the bar after he had made sure that the wee bottle was still safe in his rear pocket. "I'll give you good night."

Exe leaned on the bar, shirt-sleeves rolled above his elbows, revealing the huge, muscular arms. "Tam Bruce'll still be looking for poachers the day he dies." He eyed Donaldson shrewdly. "Is that what brought you to this part of the world? Looking for the ancestral home?"

Jay laughed. "Some ancestral home! Grandpa used to say there were two rooms, one of which was used by the sheep. . . . No, you're the one with the ancestral home, Mr. Exe. Aarolie's all I ever dreamed a Scottish castle would be." He drained his glass and pushed it over the counter. "Put another one in there for me and have one yourself."

"Thank you, sir." He poured out the whiskies and raised his drink in a salute. "Long life to you."

"Cheers! "

Hogan put the glass down. "But it wasn't only the fishing that brought you here?"

"I needed a holiday and I could afford one. For the first time in my life I could give myself a break."

Hogan agreed. "Time. That's the most important thing in life," he said vehemently, then relaxed. "And now you've got all the time in the world, eh! Time to do anything you like. . . . You'll be settling in these parts?"

"I hadn't thought of it, but I could do worse."

"Would you be going into business over here?"

There'd been an odd inflexion to Exe's words and Jay was suddenly cautious. Was the big man trying to proposition him in some way? Such as putting money into the hotel? It certainly needed some, and badly.

"What do you mean?"

"Nothing really. Just idle talk, sir."

Jay became aware of the dance tickets that he had bought and which were still lying on the bar-top. He fiddled with them, pushing them together so that one was stacked neatly on the other. Without raising his glance from the tickets, he asked, "How did you come to these parts, Mr. Exe?"

He shouldn't have asked the question. Hogan scowled, as though the words had dragged up unhappy memories. "Capitalists! "

"I beg your pardon?"

"Them damned capitalists! They ruined me, same as they ruin everyone else who gets in their clutches." Exe's mighty hands gripped the piece of cloth he had used as a bar swab and twisted it as though it was the neck of a hateful enemy. Jay shifted uncomfortably. This wasn't the genial host; the man was a stranger.

"I'm sorry. Guess I'm just poking my nose——" But he might not have spoken for all the good it did. Exe was staring fixedly over the American's shoulder, his eyes blank as though they were seeing nothing—or perhaps the past.

"Got a nice little business, we had. Father started it, but he wasn't ambitious. You know, so long as he'd got enough to eat and drink and a roof over his head . . . . But when he went I took over. And what had done for Father certainly didn't do for me. No, I was ambitious, see. I'd got big plans."

"What sort of business were you in?"

Exe ignored the question. "Big plans. But it wasn't any use. I borrowed money, see. Then, when it was all spent, they demanded their money back. I couldn't pay it; not

73

then. If they'd given me time . . . two, three years, I could have made a fortune and paid them every miserable penny I owed. But they wouldn't give me the time so I went bust.

"Capitalists!"

He spat the word out with loathing, threw down the swab and marched out from behind the bar, muttering. In the doorway he rushed past Giddon, almost knocking the fat man down. Giddon stared after the proprietor, then came into the bar chuckling.

"Our friend Exe been going on about his ruination by the filthy capitalists?"

"What gives?"

The chuckle became a laugh. "He gets like that now and again. If he really gets going he talks for hours. You can't get a word in edgeways." He climbed on to a stool beside Donaldson. "I told you the whole dam' lot of 'em are screwy."

Jay was about to make a heated retort in reply, then thought better of it. "I guess every guy has a right to his peculiarities. It'd be a dull world without 'em."

Giddon looked at him shrewdly. "An American liberal? I didn't think they were allowed to exist."

The fat man's presence was becoming objectionable. Jay got up from his seat. "There are more things in Heaven and earth, Horatio . . .!" He nodded curtly and went.

"An intellectual also?" Giddon gazed after the American complacently. "My, my! Wonders will never cease!"

The moment Jay left the bar he regretted it, for coming through the door on the opposite side of the lounge was Selina, obviously heading for the bar to take up duty behind the counter. "Hi, there!"

"Good evening, sir."

"Look, don't you ever come out from behind that protective clothing and act like a human being?"

"And how do human beings act, sir?" It was said so

74

innocently that he wasn't sure which way she meant the remark to be taken.

"I want to have a talk with you."

"I'm going to work in the bar, Mr. Donaldson. If you want to talk to me, why not have a drink there?"

"Giddon's in there."

She looked surprised. "Should that make a difference?"

"You don't mind the guy?"

"Mr. Giddon's nice. I like him."

So he'd been wrong about the fat man; obviously he wasn't the one who annoyed her. "How are your fingers? Better?"

Once again he'd said the wrong thing. She walked round him without another word and strode off, back erect, to the door of the bar. What in hell was wrong with him today? He seemed to be riling everyone he spoke to.

"Good evening, Admiral."

He looked up to see Willie peering at him from a side door. Willie had on one of his battered sailor's hats, this one had the slogan *Kiss Me Quick, I'm a Devil,* printed on the band.

"Hello, Willie."

The young man came shambling over, grinning. He seemed usually to keep out of sight. This was only the second time Jay had seen him. "You know what Constable Bruce was here for?"

"You tell me." He didn't much care for Willie's company.

"He's looking for a burglar."

"He didn't say that to me. Or your father."

"He told me though. But I didn't tell him what I knew." He giggled. "I know where the burglar is."

"You don't say!"

"I do. Honest." He came closer and whispered. "He's in the library."

"In the library? Where's that?"

"I'll show you if you want to go and catch him."

"You're joshing."

"What's that?"

"You're not telling the truth."

Willie became solemn. He held up one finger. "See that?" He drew it across his throat. "Cut my life off if I lie."

Jay looked round impatiently, hoping someone was in sight who could help him get rid of the youth. But there was no one else in the big room. "All right, Willie, that's enough." He went to push past, but was checked by the next words.

"He's got a knife and he's come to carve Selina's face." He was watching Jay slyly, the tip of his tongue sliding across his contorted mouth as he felt a warm tingle of pleasure at the expression that crossed the other man's features. "You're sweet on her!"

Did she have a crazy boy-friend? No, it was ridiculous and Jay knew it was. Even so, he couldn't risk not making absolutely certain that it was one of Willie's twisted jokes. Jay's voice was hard. "All right, show me."

Chapter Seven

WILLIE led the way to the library, pausing dramatically outside the door, finger to lips, then turned the handle and pushed the door slowly open. It was a huge, panelled room with the end wall taken up by ceiling-high, leaded windows so dirty that the evening light barely penetrated the cobweb-infested interior.

There was some shrouded furniture, chairs and tables covered with once-white cloths. The two side walls were recessed, giving dark, shadowed places that might have hidden a score of intruders. Only a few of the shelves had volumes on them, although there was space for a thousand times as many books.

Jay smiled, convinced that Willie's story wasn't true. The room looked as though no one had been in there for years. But he was interested in looking at the place. It was a noble setting, although it would have needed thousands of dollars spent to make it habitable.

"Where's your burglar, Willie?" he said lightly.

The youth turned to look at him, then pointed silently at one of the recesses in the left-hand wall.

"In there, is he?" Jay moved briskly forward. "Then we'll soon have him out." It was dark at the rear of the shallow recess, but it was possible to see that it was empty of human occupation. Jay turned. "Well, what do you know! Empty!"

Was the half-light playing tricks or was Willie's face twitching with excitement? "Here, you all right?" The youth was coming slowly towards him, eyes glittering, and was only a foot away.

"He's right behind you, Mister." The words were whispered as though Willie didn't want them to be overheard.

"Don't be——" He moved a step backwards and twisted to avoid Willie's steady approach.

"He's right behind you!"

The youth skipped to one side and crouched down as though to avoid attack and Jay felt something iron-hard ram into his spine. *"One move and I'll blow your guts out!"* The voice was a grating bass, hollow-sounding and frightening.

For a moment Jay froze, then Willie gave a screech of laughter, straightened himself upright and went pelting out of the room. Jay stared after him then spun round to face the blank panelling. "You little son of a——" He ran his fingers over the wood, but could find nothing to account for the blow he had received in the back.

He looked thoughtfully at the spot where Willie had crouched, then went down on hands and knees to see if he could find anything. It took very little time to locate the operating device. A small square of wood in the skirting board sank in under pressure and as he pushed it he heard a click. In the back of the recess an oblong piece of panel flicked aside and a piece of timber shot out. At the end of the timber was what appeared to be a gloved hand, holding a gun.

"One move and I'll blow your guts out!" It was the same, menacing voice and when he removed the pressure from the square of skirting board the gun disappeared and the panel closed. When he pressed it again the whole process was repeated. *"One move and I'll blow your guts out!"*

He let his breath out in a sigh of relief. Even though he hadn't believed Willie's story, the youth had certainly succeeded in frightening him momentarily. He stood up and absent-mindedly brushed the dust from his trouser legs. The device was ingenious; it was a pity Willie couldn't spend his energies on something more profitable .

Jay stared round the room then went across to the

nearest shelf where there were some books. Selecting one large, leather-bound volume he carried it towards the light, brushing the dust off it so that he could read the embossed title:

A HISTORY OF DEVILS, WITCHES AND NECROMANCY

Mrs. Exe was at her dressing-table, trying to get the mantilla of Queen Isabella's court dress to sit correctly, but none of the positions to which she moved it satisfied her.

Hogan was striding up and down the room behind her, muttering to himself and scowling. "Do sit down, dear, you'll tire yourself out."

"How can I sit down when there's so much injustice in the world, Mother? I mean, I ought to be out, doing something to put it right."

"You'll get your chance with Mr. Donaldson," she said soothingly.

"Every capitalist in the world ought to have his money confiscated. They're the cause of all the unhappiness in the world."

"Yes, dear." She tried the mantilla again, without success.

"Crushing good men down."

"Yes, dear." Maybe if she tried it tilted the other way?

"I'd like to kill the lot of 'em."

"Don't get too excited, Hoagy, you know it isn't good for your liver."

"If I'd got ten million pounds, *I* wouldn't be a capitalist. I'd do *good*."

"Of course you would, my son." There, that was better. "Did you get that wire I asked for?"

"I'd do good. Real good."

"Yes, dear." She added one or two touches and stared at her reflection admiringly. "Did you get the wire?"

He stopped pacing. "What wire?"

"The wire I asked you to get. You know."

"Oh, that!" His face lost some of its bitterness. "I've told Willie to get some to-morrow."

She turned to face him. "Where are you sending him?"

"MacIntyre."

"That's a good boy. He hasn't been there this year."

He was slightly indignant. "Mother, you surely don't think I'd send him back to the same place too often? Tam Bruce'd soon smell a rat if we bought bale after bale of wire from Hannay's Stores."

"I just wanted to be sure, Hoagy."

"Yes, I know, Ma." His depression was gone; now he was sulking. "I'm sorry you can't trust me. Your own son."

"Silly boy, of course I do!" She smiled lovingly at him. "I'm just waiting for you to say the word about Mr. Donaldson."

He paused, nodding thoughtfully. "I'm almost certain he'll join the Club. Question is, should we move him into the special room now, or wait a bit."

"I've been thinking about this, Hoagy."

"Yes, Mother?"

"I looked all through his luggage and I read all the papers he's got with him. He's genuine—doesn't know a soul in this country, no relatives, single . . ."

"I know all that. I saw it myself."

"He's a very rich man, son."

"I know that too."

"If you buy a keg of butter you don't eat an ounce and throw the rest away. Not if it's first-class butter, in prime condition. . . . If you buy a case of Scotch, Hoagy, you don't pour the rest of it in the loch after you've had one sip."

"What are you getting at, Mother?"

She made a deprecatory gesture. "Only this, son. Mr. Donaldson's a rich man. He's retired, a millionaire. So how does he get his money?"

Hogan was puzzled. "What do you mean?"

"I mean, maybe Mr. White would like a companion. Maybe that way you'd be able to get more of Mr. Donaldson's money?"

He thought it over for a few moments then nodded his head vigorously. "Regular payments? Could be." He went to where she was sitting and stooped to kiss her cheek. "I'll think about it."

His caress had knocked the mantilla slightly out of true and she put it straight. "There's another thing, dear. . . . If you've got a waste disposal unit fitted in the sink, you don't leave bones in the dustbin."

"Well?"

"We've got a perfectly good disposal unit fitted in the special room.

"So?"

"So why don't we give that room to Mr. Donaldson. He can stay there as long as it takes you to decide what's to be done."

"Why?"

"Hoagy, my son, sometimes I think you'll never make a good man of business. Don't you see, dear? If he's in that room you could charge him more for accommodation. The room's not earning anything while it's empty."

He was enchanted. "I'll see him right away, Mother."

The bar was empty except for Selina when Jay returned, and he wasted no time in getting down to trying to date her. Pulling the tickets from his pocket, he placed them on the bar-top so that she could read them.

"How about a date?"

She looked at the tickets, then turned the clear regard of her blue eyes on him. "I don't understand."

"I'm asking if you'll go to the hop with me." He held up his arms as though holding a dancing partner, grinning and executing a few exaggerated steps. "You know, dancing?"

Suddenly she was a little breathless and her eyes shone. A dance! She hadn't been to one for . . . how long was it? Jay was watching her expectantly. "Well, what do you say?" he demanded.

"I—Friday's not possible, I'm afraid, Mr. Donaldson. But it was very kind of you to ask me."

"Look. Is it me? . . . I mean, would you object to going with me?"

"Of course not."

"Well, I'll warn you I'm not much good at it. Once a year, that's all I went. The Company dance." He shook his head in mock sorrow. "Brother! Preserve me from that sort of thing ever again."

Selina was about to comment, then changed her mind The momentary sparkle had gone from her face. "Did you want a drink, sir?"

He looked at her sharply. "Is it 'no'?" She kept her head bent, refusing to look at him. "Why isn't Friday possible? You got another date?" Still she kept silent, fiddling miserably with a glass drying cloth. "Well, if it isn't that, what is it?" He was getting angry. If there'd been some sort of response from her he wouldn't have minded, but to have her withdraw into silence simply made him mad.

At any moment some other person might come into the bar and spoil his chance of talking privately with Selina. "Is that it? Another date?"

At last she looked up at him. "I shall be working."

"You get *some* time off, surely?"

"Well, of course."

"Then switch. I'll ask your Uncle, if you like."

"Ask her Uncle what?"

Jay spun round to see Exe coming towards him, smiling broadly. There was nothing left of the former, odd mood. The proprietor looked jovial and Jay took advantage of the fact. "I was asking Selina to go to that dance with me on Friday."

Hogan smiled his approval. "You'll enjoy yourself, my dear," he said to the girl. "Do you good to get away for a bit." He turned back to the American. "She works too hard, you know."

"I haven't got anything I could wear."

"Then buy yourself a dress, my girl. Willie's going in to —to do some shopping in the morning. You could go with him."

The prospect of being alone with Willie was not a happy one and Jay sensed her apprehension. "Look, I want to do some shopping in the morning. I'll be driving into the nearest town. Why not come with me?"

She looked uncertainly at Exe, but he was still in an amiable mood. "Will that be all right, Uncle? I mean, if Willie's off duty as well . . .?"

"We can manage, don't you fret. . . . Enjoy yourself while you can, lass. None of us lives for ever, do we, Mr. Donaldson? Take your pleasures while you're young enough to enjoy 'em, that's what I always say." He sighed deeply. "None of us knows if he's going to be cut down tomorrow." For several moments he contemplated the uncertainty of life gloomily, then brightened. "Well, now that's settled, there's another thing I wanted to mention to you, sir."

"Yes?"

"I've had a cancellation, and I was wondering if you'd like to move into the room? It's much better than the one you've got at the moment."

"O.K., show me. Then I'll tell you if I want to move."

"If you'd like to come now?"

"Sure." He turned to Selina with a smile. "Don't go 'way, now. I'll be back."

He followed the bearded man up the grand staircase and turned left at the top. Half a minute later he gasped in surprise as Exe held open a door and switched on some lights. "What a magnificent room!" He stared round in appreciation, then grinned. "I shouldn't make myself so obvious, should I! You'll be making me pay through the nose."

"I'm afraid the rate *is* rather higher, sir."

"How much higher?"

Hogan coughed delicately. "Double, sir."

Jay looked in at the bathroom, then went over to the four-poster. "Is this the genuine article?"

"I guarantee it, sir."

"Well, what do you know!" He eyed it speculatively, touching the scroll-work on one of the posts. "It's Tudor, isn't it?"

"Elizabethan—the first Elizabeth, that is. But it's most comfortable, sir. I can thoroughly recommend it. I've slept in it myself, many a time."

"You'll not be the only one, Mr. Exe. . . . Four hundred years old, eh?"

"At least. Yes, a lot of people have slept in that bed—a lot of people have been born in it."

Jay smiled. "What about those who have died in it?" he asked slyly.

Hogan didn't bat an eyelid. "We never talk about those, sir," he said coyly.

Donaldson gave a hoot of laughter. "I'll bet you don't! . . . But you've got yourself another customer, Exe. As of now, this room's mine."

Exe bowed slightly. "I thought you'd like it. And I think you'll find you'll sleep soundly in the bed. It might take a bit to get used to it, but when you do finally drop off, I guarantee you won't wake up in a hurry."

But the American was not paying attention; he was examining the hand-carving again, running his fingertips round a curve in the design. "Beautiful workmanship! Is it one of the original pieces?"

"Good lord, no! The castle was built three hundred years before that bed was made. No, we bought it when we inherited the place."

"Inherited? Does that make you a lord or something?"

"No, nothing like that. We didn't inherit through blood-ties, sir." He hesitated, as though wondering whether to confide any further, then went on: "When I was robbed out of my business, Mother and I came up here to work for the man who owned the place. It was a private residence in those days. The owner thought highly of Mother and me—Willie was only a boy. So when the poor gentleman died, we found he'd left the place to us."

"I see." It looked to Jay as though the other man was eager to continue the conversation and, as he didn't want Exe to reverse his decision about giving Selina time off, Jay encouraged him. "Did you work for him long?" Not that he wanted to know, but it was the only question he could think of to ask.

"Nearly two years."

"Really?" It seemed a very short space of time for which to show such gratitude.

"It was a terrible blow, losing Mr. Green. Such a nice young gentleman."

"Young?" Jay had assumed the dead man to be elderly, at least.

"About your own age, sir. It was an accident. Some of the stonework on the battlement was rotten and poor Mr. Green fell off." Exe shook his head mournfully at the recollection. "Of course, he shouldn't have been up there in the first place, but he was stubborn. Stubborn as a Cairo donkey."

Jay waited a moment for the other man to continue, realizing he was going to have to listen to the whole story. Resigned, he asked the obvious question and Hogan took up the tale briskly.

"He shouldn't have been there because he was a cripple. Couldn't walk properly, *shouldn't* have walked up on the battlements. But I suppose he had to prove he wasn't help-less. That's what I told the police. Mr. Green knew the battlements were dangerous; there's a lot of the castle I've had to shut off, so that the guests don't get into an accident. It isn't safe, and that's a fact, in some parts." Hogan smiled, to make the words seem friendly. "So let that be a lesson to you, sir. Don't go wandering. We'd hate to lose you that way."

The American grinned. "You won't get rid of me that easily, Exe."

Hogan was equally affable. "In that case, sir, we'll have to think of something else."

The hotel's tiny bar was doing good business, with four of the guests who had been playing bridge now taking their last drinks for the night. Selina attended to them, giving less than her usual attention to the job. Would the good-looking American return as he had promised? Or had what he'd said been idle chatter? Did he really mean it about the dance? She experienced a flutter of excitement when he came in at the door.

Three of the stools were occupied and he propped himself up on the fourth. "I hope you're going to buy a blue dress tomorrow."

"There might not be anything I like in blue." She hesitated, unsure of herself. "It—it's very kind of you to take me into the town, Mr. Donaldson."

"It'll be a pleasure."

"You're sure it won't be a nuisance? I—we'll have to start off early. I'll have to be back to serve lunch."

"Back for lunch?" He'd planned to take her to the best hotel he could find and treat her. "I thought all the guests were off fishing all day?"

"We get tourists dropping in for a meal."

"Couldn't someone else look after them for once?"

"It's my job, Mr. Donaldson." Her voice had more determination in it than he'd heard previously. She'd spoken the words in sharp reproof, as though he'd suggested she should do something wrong.

"O.K., O.K., I'm sorry!" He held up his hands in mock surrender. "So what time shall we leave?"

"Whatever time suits you, sir."

She was the timid servant once more and he was irritated by the rapid switch of personality. "After breakfast?"

"Very well, sir."

"O.K." He stood up. "Good night." It was impossible to say anything of a private nature to her with the other men in the bar; he'd leave all that until the morning.

He took the grand staircase two steps at a time and went to go right at the top, then remembered and turned in the opposite direction. His new room gave him a fresh thrill when he entered. There was a small fire in the enormous fireplace, serving to make it look even more attractive. Exe, or Willie, had transferred all Jay's things from the old room and his pyjamas were laid out on the four-poster.

On the dressing-table there was a whisky bottle, a glass jug filled with water and a napkin-covered plate that proved to be filled with delicately-cut sandwiches. He poured himself a drink, tried one of the sandwiches and nodded appreciatively at his reflection in the mirror.

"They're certainly giving you the works, boy," he said aloud to himself. Stretching, he began to undress.

Jay took a bath then got ready for bed. There were a few novels in one of his suitcases and he brought the books out to select one to read, then climbed into the four-poster and settled down.

Willie, crouched down in the corridor outside to look through Jay's keyhole, saw the main lights switched off inside the room. Now there was only the glow that he knew came from the reading-light beside the bed. Satisfied, he straightened and ran down to the entrance-hall, letting himself out at the front door.

In the faint moonlight he took a cap from his pocket and put it on his head with the peak at the rear. Then, looking up to check that no lights were showing, he ran round to the huge lean-to where the cars were kept. It took a minute's work under the bonnet of the silver-grey Bentley to start the engine, then, climbing into the driving seat he backed the car out, turned it and drove off down the narrow track that led to the road.

A minute later he was shouting with excitement as the needle of the speedometer passed the eighty mark, the huge car's headlights throwing a brilliant beam of light along the road ahead as its engine hurled it, almost silently, along the twisting road.

At a bend that was sharper than those he had passed already, he had to jerk the wheel hard, fighting it for mastery. The car, tyres screaming, kept on the road by a miracle, slewing across to the offside, its wheels not more than six inches from the edge of a fifty-foot sheer drop where the mountain-side fell away from the road.

Chapter Eight

MRS. EXE was always first up and this morning was no exception. From the window of her bedroom she looked out at the sky. Grey clouds were gathering; it looked as though the fine spell was coming to an end. She would have to remember to tell Willie to drive carefully while he was out. Sometimes the dear child was inclined to drive too fast. If it rained, the roads would be dangerous.

"Shaving!"

She bustled down to the kitchen and prepared a breakfast tray then trotted down to see Mr. White. He was still asleep when she reached him, his body and head slumped over as far as his bonds would allow. She switched on the desk light.

"Wakey, wakey! Time to get up!"

From out of the capacious pocket of her overall she took an electric razor, plugging it into a socket and placing the razor itself on the flat surface just within his reach. "Come on, now!"

Slowly his eyelids lifted and then he was immediately awake. "Good morning, Mr. White. Looks as though we're going to have some rain, doesn't it?"

Without paying her any attention he picked up the razor, switched it on and began to shave. When he had cleared most of the stubble from his face he switched off, replaced the razor and reached up to grab the pulley chain. A moment later he was moving sideways, watched by the gently approving Mrs. Exe. "That's right." She took the razor, unplugged it and put it back into her overall pocket, then pushed the tray to where White could reach it when he returned.

There was a great deal of work to be done and she had better go and get on with it. She went into the next cellar and paused by the door waiting. The noise of a w.c. flushing made itself heard and she nodded, satisfied.

"Good boy!"

She was humming the first bars of *Lead, kindly light* as she went up to prepare breakfast for the other guests.

Willie woke at the usual time, reaching out a hand to pick up a hat that bore the legend *I like Sex* and clapping it on his head. It was the first move in the daily routine.

Next came the business of the seven darts. They were kept in a case under his pillow and he fished them out, lying back and making an aiming point by poking his toes up under the bedclothes at the foot of the bunk. First he pushed his feet apart, the toes out at an angle of about forty-five degrees. Then, slowly, he brought the toes of each foot towards the other until his feet were upright, coverlet sagging between them.

Lying back on the pillows, he threw the darts, aiming them to pass between his shrouded feet and fall to the floor beyond the end of the bunk. The seven darts discharged, he climbed down from the bunk and went to see where they had fallen. Two of them had pierced a sheet of typewritten paper he had placed on the floor before going to sleep the previous night, and one of the two was actually sticking up in a typed sentence.

"It will be a good day," he read out, grinning.

Stripping off his pyjama jacket and revealing a fleshy chest, he went to the wash-basin and examined his face critically in the mirror, rubbing his hand several times across his jaw, then setting to work with shaving soap and brush. He worked up a lather, then regarded the result in the glass, shaking his head doubtfully and swilling off all the lather again.

Next time he did the job properly; the white, soapy mess

was thick enough to meet with his approval. Then, solemnly and with great concentration, he began to scrape at the lather carefully, using the outstretched forefinger of his right hand as though it was the blade of an open razor. With all the lather removed, he examined his reflection again and beamed happily.

Selina held up the dress on its hanger and looked at it critically, it was worn, but not really shabby yet. Would one of the other two be better to wear that morning? She looked them both over then went back to the first one; though older, it had been the most expensive of the three; she would feel more confident if some snooty salesgirl helped her take it off when she was trying on the new one. She laid the dress out ready on the bed.

Although the sky was overcast, to her it was a much brighter morning. It would be marvellous to get away from the castle for an hour or two. Sometimes she felt she couldn't stand the place another minute.

She took off the worn dressing-gown and began to put on the black dress and frilly white apron she used when she waited at table. That morning, even the uniform looked good. As she smoothed the apron into place and twisted sideways to examine the outline of her figure in the looking-glass, she began to sing under her breath.

Whistling, Jay ran down the main staircase. Hogan Exe was in the hall, taking the letters from the post-box, ready for when the mail van arrived. "You off now, Mr. Donaldson?"

"Yeah. I'm just waiting for Selina."

"Doesn't look as though the weather's going to hold."

"It won't hurt the fishing, will it?"

Exe smiled. "*Nothing* spoils the fishing here, my dear fellow. Except, perhaps, my niece? You know, you're the first guest we've ever had who's given up a day's sport to go into the town."

Jay looked at Exe closely. Was the guy getting at him? Perhaps it would be better to ignore the crack—if it was one. He heard the sound of high heels clicking over the granite floor and turned to find Selina coming towards him. She was wearing a white trench coat, belted tightly, that showed how slender her waist was. She had brushed out her blonde, shoulder-length hair; it made a bright frame round her sweet face. Jay forgot everything else as he looked at her.

"Ready? . . . O.K., let's go." He took her elbow and steered her towards the door.

They walked out under the sardonic gaze of Hogan Exe. The moment they were out of sight he looked through the few letters he held. One of them was addressed to someone in New York and after looking round to make certain he was not observed, Exe slipped the letter into the inside pocket of his tweed jacket.

Jay and Selina walked round to the lean-to where the guests' cars were garaged. Jay opened the near-side door for Selina to get in, settled her and went round to the driving seat. He had just put the ignition key in when he frowned.

"That's funny! "

"What is?"

He was looking at the speedometer. It was showing a total of twelve miles more than when he had last seen it— and he wasn't making a mistake. "When I put the car away" —he indicated the speedometer mileage figure—"this was showing an odd three miles. Naught, three. But now it shows fifteen."

"How could that happen?"

"I don't know." He managed a smile. "Maybe I'm mistaken. It doesn't matter, anyway." It certainly wasn't worth spoiling the morning over, but he knew he hadn't made a mistake. Checking the total mileage of his car at the end of a day's run was a habit—maybe it was a silly habit, but at least it was a harmless one.

He switched on, and backed out until he'd got space to turn, doing it with a flourish that he realized was meant to impress the girl sitting beside him. But she wasn't interested in his driving; the fingers of her right hand were caressing the luxurious leather upholstery. As he drove down the narrow track to the road she turned to him, her eyes alight with pleasure.

"I've never been in a car like this before. It—it's beautiful." There was no envy in her voice, just pure admiration for the magnificence of the car and its appointments.

"You like it, eh?"

"Don't you?"

"I reckon the best's good enough for me." Immediately he'd said the words he regretted them; it was a stupid, boastful thing to say to someone who, from her clothes, quite obviously had little money to spend. "You enjoy speed?"

"I don't know. I've never thought about it."

"Well, we'll have to see, won't we?"

Out on the open road he pushed the car up to seventy, sparing a glance now and again for the girl. Even at that speed the streamlining of the windscreen kept her hair undisturbed, but some colour had whipped into her cheeks and her eyes were shining. "Enjoying it?"

"It's marvellous! "

He eased his toe on the accelerator as they approached a sharp bend. Beyond it the road curved and he kept the speed down until, ahead, he saw a lone cyclist. A moment later he recognized the man as Bruce, the local policeman. Tam must have heard the noise of their tyres on the road surface—he certainly couldn't have heard the engine for it was silent—he looked back over his shoulder, then stopped and dismounted, waving them down.

"Good morning, sir, good morning, lassie." He touched his cap as Jay pulled up.

"Were we breaking the speed limit?"

"No, sir, I just wanted a wee word with you." He eyed the American solemnly. "You wouldn't have been out and about last night?"

"No."

"Ah, a pity. Selina, ma girl, tell your Uncle I'll be up to see him the night."

"Is anything wrong?"

Bruce drew closer, dropping his voice to a whisper as though not to be overheard, despite the fact that apart from the three of them, the mountain-side, the road and the valley on their right were deserted. "They were oot last night!"

Selina glanced at Jay, then turned back to the policeman. "You mean the poachers?"

"Aye!"

"How do you know?" Jay asked.

"I saw 'em!" Tam was triumphant. For the first time he had proof, actual proof, that the poachers existed outside his own imagination. Unfortunately, it wasn't proof that his sergeant was prepared to accept, for his superior was blind to the truth.

"Only *saw* them?"

"Aye!" Some of the policeman's exuberance faded. "Och, they must be highly organized. They were coming down this very road, headlights blazing and tearing along as though Beelzebub himself was after them. I was going to stop them, make an arrest, but they stopped their car, turned round and made off." He shook his head sadly. "If they'd kept on another mile, I'd have got them red-handed!"

"Bad luck."

"Oh, aye. But I'll have them, I'll have them. . . . I wanted to know if you'd heard anything, or seen anything, last night. Strangers . . . shots . . . anything."

"What time?"

"Aboot midnight."

"Not me, Mr. Bruce," Jay stated. "Sorry."

"Nor me, I'm afraid," Selina said.

"Ah well, I'll have them, I'll have them."

He saluted them as Jay started up and Selina twisted round to stare at him as he faded into the distance behind them. "I wonder if there's any truth in what he says?"

"About poachers? Why?"

"I just wondered." There was something in the way she spoke that made him uncertain.

"You know something?"

"Me?" She laughed. "Good lord, no!" It was the first time he had heard her laugh and he badly wanted to hear the sound again.

"I'll bet you're the chief of the gang," he said flippantly.

"How did you guess!" She was responding very well to his light-hearted jesting.

"Mysterious blonde heads gang of poachers." He said it as though quoting a newspaper headline.

"Mysterious? What's mysterious about me?" She seemed genuinely puzzled.

"Everything. I don't know anything about you. Where you come from, who your folks are . . . anything." He waited, but she wasn't to be drawn. Had he offended her? He'd try one more cast. "I can't even place your accent."

She stared at him, her blue eyes wide. "Accent? Do I have an *accent*?"

"Of course."

"Well!" She sounded rueful. "I thought I spoke English."

"You're English, then?"

"What did you think I was? Chinese?"

He slowed the car to a crawl. "Look, I don't mind what you are. . . ."

"Thank you, that's very tolerant of you."

He was annoyed with himself. He didn't seem able to handle the situation at all. Jay Donaldson, the guy who had the reputation of being the smartest operator within a radius of a hundred miles of his home town! Maybe he'd

95

better try again, and this time be somewhat more diplomatic. He turned to her, she was looking away across the valley; the curve of her cheek was appealing, the veil of bright hair lying softly against it.

"I'm sorry. What I meant, was, you don't sound exactly Scottish. There's some sort of turn to your speech at times. . . ."

"I lived in Northern Ireland when I was a child," she said abruptly. He looked at her as she sat there erect, and from the set of her mouth he judged it wise to drop the whole subject.

"What sort of dress are you going to buy?"

"I don't know, Mr. Donaldson, and I won't know until I've seen the one I like and can afford." She spoke coldly, as though giving an explanation to a child she didn't much care for. Maybe he'd better keep his big mouth shut, for a while at least.

Willie was enjoying his trip much more. Not that he was really satisfied, for the old shooting-brake couldn't manage more than a bare sixty, even when he pushed his foot on the accelerator so hard that it almost went through the floorboards. He was covering the same stretch of road he'd driven along when he went for his joy-ride in the silver-grey Bentley, but with only one-quarter of the comfort and three-quarters of the speed. Even so he was going too fast for the road and when he wrenched the wheel round to negotiate the bends the tyres squealed in protest.

When he reached the spot when he had to turn sharp right he flung the shooting-brake into the corner and for a moment screamed with pleasure as he felt the off-side wheels lift clear from the ground. The vehicle righted itself, the rear doors flying open as the tyres bumped back on the road.

Grinning, he stopped and went round to the rear of the brake to fasten the doors securely, then he accelerated madly away, trying to make up for the lost seconds. Half a mile farther on he passed a car coming from the opposite direction and made its driver jerk savagely at his steering-wheel to avoid a collision.

At the outskirts of the town where he was going to do his shopping, Willie became a sedate driver, his speed well below the limit allowed. He gave exaggerated hand signals and waved other motorists on deferentially. He parked in the yard of the Station Hotel and consulted his shopping-list.

It took him an hour to buy all he had to; now it was time to sneak into the hotel. He wandered in, making sure that no one was about, and looking round the small entrance-hall without seeing what he wanted. At the MacIntyre Arms, farther along the street, he tried again. This time he found a sign painted on a door—"Writing Room". Cautiously he looked inside.

The place was empty and he went in swiftly, going over to the tables by the window were there were racks of stationery. He bent to examine the contents of one of the racks and after making sure no one had come in, helped himself to some postcards, putting them into his inside pocket and walking out, whistling.

Jay parked the Bentley and switched off the engine. He looked at his watch. "Right. I'll meet you back here in a couple of hours—unless you'd like me to come and help you choose a dress?" He looked hopeful.

"No, thank you, I know just what I want." Her tone was very firm.

He touched a strand of the silken hair that lay on her shoulder. "I know, why don't you get a few yards of sea-weed and go as a water nymph." According to the ticket it was a fancy-dress dance, though Tam Bruce had said not many people attended in costume.

97

She laughed delightedly, then looked serious. "No, since I'm taking the plunge, I may as well get something I can wear pretty often."

Much as he wanted to, he didn't make the mistake of offering to help with money, or even to make a present of the dress. "All right. Two hours?"

"An hour and a half."

"Very well. I don't mind what colour it is, as long as it's blue. . . . My favourite."

"Yes, sir, I'll see what I can find." For a moment she looked as though she was going to break into laughter again, but then she turned and walked quickly away.

Jay was satisfied with a quick walk up and down the main shopping street. The town was ugly, the granite buildings lacking in charm. The mountain peaks were too distant to provide an impressive backcloth. But the place was busy enough, with obvious tourists strolling aimlessly up and down. He settled down in the Bentley to wait for Selina.

It gave him a curious sense of well-being and transient security when he saw Selina coming towards him, carrying a package. He scrambled out of the car. "You've done your shopping already?"

She nodded, bright-eyed. "The very first thing I saw!" It had cost more than she'd intended to pay, but she could put the money back if she saved extra hard within the next few weeks.

"What a woman! Am I going to see it?"

"Not until Friday."

He took the package from her and put it on the back seat of the car. She looked completely different, transformed, as though . . . he regarded her intently, wondering how he would define the change. As though some burden had been lifted from her.

"How about some coffee?"

"Please. I'd love a cup."

98

They tried the biggest hotel and found surprising service. A dark-eyed, plump waitress took their order and was back in seconds with a loaded tray. The room was small, panelled with oak that was almost black with age. Selina took off her gloves to pour the coffee and on the first three fingers of her right hand he saw the purple marks of the bruising.

"Your fingers stopped hurting?"

As soon as he had asked the question he cursed himself. All her new-found confidence vanished. She snatched her injured hand out of sight and reverted to the almost frightened girl he had seen when first he arrived at Aarolie Castle.

There was a moment of strained silence between them, then he leaned forward and took hold of her right arm, pulling it towards him until he could clasp her hand. His grip was gentle as he turned the back of her hand upwards and passed the fingertips of his other hand over the bruised flesh.

"How did it happen?" he asked softly.

She was struggling to pull her hand free. "Please!" she begged. "It—it was an accident."

But he was determined to get at the truth. "Someone did that to you, didn't they!" His voice was deep and gentle as he stared at her, looking her straight in the eyes. "Didn't they!"

"It—it was an accident." She was pale now and trembling, not making any further effort to get free.

"I don't think it was."

Her breast was rising and falling jerkily as she strove for control. Her blue eyes were completely clear of guile as they gazed into his. "It was an accident. I—I caught my fingers in a mousetrap."

It was so obviously true that he was taken aback. "Why didn't you say so!"

There was colour in her cheeks now as she lowered her

gaze. "It—it isn't the sort of thing you let the guests know about," she whispered.

Jay sat back, miserably conscious of the fact that he'd made an idiot of himself and not much caring for the sensation.

Chapter Nine

THE long-threatened rain began to fall as they left the town. Jay closed the hood and they drove on into the gathering storm, with thunder booming all round them. In a way, Donaldson was grateful for the noise of the elements; at least it made conversation inside the car too difficult to attempt. The rain was lashing down and flashes of searing, purple light streaked across the leaden sky.

They were leaving the level moorland now, the road running between rising walls of granite, with inches of water covering its surface. As one particularly vivid lightning flash seemed almost to be reaching out to strike them, Jay glanced quickly at the girl. She was sitting quietly, hunched as far away as she could get from him, but she was looking out indifferently at the storm.

Between the rolling echoes of the thunder he called out. "You're all right?" She glanced at him questioningly. "You're not scared of lightning?"

She moved her shoulders as though in disdain. "I'm used to it."

He bit his lip in annoyance. In her presence, all his normal quota of intelligence appeared to desert him until he became the world's prize idiot.

The storm was brief and violent. Fifteen minutes after it had begun the sky was clear and the sun shining on a streaming world. There was one consolation, he wouldn't have missed much in the way of fishing; the water would be too dirty to do much now, and for the rest of the day at least.

Willie was more fortunate with the weather. As he drew

near Aarolie he could see, in the distance, the heavy grey clouds that shrouded the mountains half-way down and heard the growling rumble of thunder. But where he was the road was dry; no rain had fallen. It was his last chance to do a bit of fast driving and he put his toe down hard.

Ahead of him, a speck in the distance, he could see someone. He identified Tam Bruce even though he was still far away. The constable was at the T-junction, leaning on his bicycle and probably dreaming about catching poachers. Willie chuckled. He'd show the copper what a brilliant driver Willie Exe was.

Hunched over the wheel, Willie held his speed until it seemed inevitable that he would be unable to make the turn and go ploughing on to smash the policeman down. But at the very last moment he half-steered, half-skidded the shooting-brake round the right-angled bend and sped away, laughing at the expression on Tam's face as the officer leapt back in alarm.

As the vehicle recovered from the terrific force of cornering, Willie heard an odd noise behind him. The drum of wire that had been behind the driving seat, rolled backwards and crashed into the rear door, forcing it open. The drum dropped to the road, skidding wildly along behind the brake before shooting off on to the verge and coming to rest.

Willie accepted the unavoidable. Grinning, he stopped, then reversed to where the drum was lying, and got out. He turned to leer at the policeman as Tam puffed up on his bicycle. "Don't you reckon I should be a racing driver, Mr. Bruce?"

"I should give you a summons for dangerous driving," Tam said sourly.

"I wasn't driving dangerously, Mr. Bruce. I wouldn't have done it if there'd been any other cars about. You know that."

Bruce didn't. What he did know was that Willie was a

explosion.

"What?"

Exe was unperturbed. "I said, it's a funny thing. Chaps building a place like this so it would last for centuries, when they themselves didn't know if they were going to live through the week."

"They built for security. It's what we all want."

"Security? . . . Yes, of course. As you say, Mr. Donaldson, we all want it. But very few of us are as lucky as you are, sir."

"Lucky?" Jay was indignant. "There wasn't much luck about what I've done. I had to work for everything I earned. Work like a slave. Worse than any varlet, or whatever you call 'em, who sweated in this place back in history."

Hogan seemed to be intent on his cigar ash. "Don't you believe in luck sir? Good luck? Bad luck?"

Jay opened his mouth to make a hasty comment, then closed it. He thought about the other man's question for a moment, then gave in. "I wouldn't deny there *is* such a thing as luck," he said at last. "But a man who relied on luck to get what he wanted . . . ?"

"Good point, sir. . . . Know what you want, then set out to get it for yourself, eh?"

"Something like that."

"Yes. . . . But you can try all you like and if the luck's against you . . ."

It was quite a different argument to the one Exe had put up on a previous occasion and Jay wondered what would happen if he reminded the hotel proprietor of his former comments about capitalists. But before he could make up his mind he saw Mrs. Exe enter the room and come over to the window, beaming.

"Isn't it a *lovely* storm! "

She had a bundle of knitting with her and she sat down at a table near the window, settling herself comfortably and starting to get the wool sorted out.

"Hoagy, darling, I think I'd like a cup of tea. And I'm sure Mr. Donaldson would as well." She looked up at him, the lines on her face creasing more deeply as she smiled. "You wouldn't say no to a cup?"

"It would be delightful."

"Splendid. Hoagy, dear . . . ?" Without a word he went off and she patted the seat beside her own. "Now, sit down, my boy." She looked at him with affection. " 'It would be delightful.' . . . You said that almost as well as an Englishman would."

"Do I take that as a compliment?"

She twinkled at him. "Now don't you make fun of a poor old woman! I meant what I said. I think you've got English blood—English relations perhaps?" Her knitting was going well now and she didn't appear to have to give it any attention for her movements were automatic.

"My old Grandad was Scottish. That's the nearest I can claim to any British connexions, I guess."

"Ah, yes, was it Hoagy who told me your people came from these parts?" She shook her head. "I can't recall who told me, but no matter. Personally, you'll never convince me that you have any connexion with *this* part of the country."

"Why not, Mrs. Exe?"

"Because you're too—too gentle, that's why."

Jay laughed. "None of my business competitors ever said that of me."

"Then they didn't know you." Over the tops of her glasses she regarded him mildly. "And you couldn't have ancestors from these parts because those old Scottish clansmen were terrible. Just dreadful!"

"I know. My old Grandad used to tell me about the clan wars. I guess there was a lot of blood spilt."

"My dear boy, I doubt if you've heard a hundredth part of what went on. Why, in this very castle——" She stopped, as though she had said too much, but his curiosity had been roused.

"Something happened here?"

Mrs. Exe put her knitting down on the table and stared at him solemnly. "Mr. Donaldson, if you knew some of the things that went on here, your blood would run cold." Aggravatingly, she took up her knitting again and gave it all her attention. "Oooh! Wasn't that a lovely flash! . . . I like to watch the storms, you know. I mean, all that violence outside and here I am, safe and snug *inside*."

He could have taken her sweet old neck in his two hands and strangled her. "Mrs. Exe, *what* took place here?"

"Here?" All her habitual vagueness was in her face and tone.

"You—you said that *things* went on . . . ?"

"Ask Hoagy. He knows all the history of Aarolie."

And with that he had to be content until Exe returned, wheeling a tea-wagon, the old woman giving a cry of pleasure at the sight of him. "Ah, tea!"

For a moment Jay had the illusion that he was a guest of a family. Mrs. Exe dispensed the cups of tea with a grace and ease of manner that he found impressive. Before coming to Scotland he had never drunk the stuff, but now he was beginning to like it. When she had served them, Mrs. Exe looked fondly at her son.

"I was telling Mr. Donaldson that Aarolie has quite a history."

"Yes."

Jay was determined to know the story. "Your Mother made it sound quite sinister."

"Oh, it was. There used to be some dreadful things go on. . . . Take the second Robert. He was the chap who finished building this place. His father started it but didn't live to see it more than begun. Auld Rabbie! Now there was a character. . . . That room you're sleeping in, Mr. Donaldson. Immediately above that is part of what used to be called the Great Dining Hall."

107

"On the *second* floor?" Jay looked at the other man with suspicion.

"I know it's unusual, but there's a reason for it. . . . Auld Rabbie used to seat his guests at table so they were more or less over the bit above your room. They'd eat, then he'd start proposing toasts, and when they were all a bit fuddled, and on their feet for another toast, he'd give a signal to his executioner and half the damned floor used to drop down on a great hinge, and stop at such a steep angle that all the guests slid over the edge."

Hogan gave a deep, chuckling laugh, his face lit by a flare of lightning. "They'd all go over the edge, into a hole that fell sheer into the dungeons below—all of eighty feet on to the granite."

In the darkened room the story made Jay's scalp crawl and he shivered, picturing the frightful scene. He moistened his lips. "What happened then?"

"Auld Rabbie's troops picked up the bodies, looted what they wanted from them, then carried them to a chute that had been cut through the solid rock. It opened out at the other end, over the waters of the loch." Exe settled back, watching the other man to see what effect the tale had had. "Not a bad way of disposing of unwanted guests, eh?"

"Ghastly! "

Exe's shoulders were shaking with laughter. "Maybe all those bodies were what the trout fed on, Mr. Donaldson. I mean, there must be some reason for them growing to such a size."

Jay didn't find the remark amusing. He looked at Mrs. Exe, but she showed no sign of revulsion; she was staring down at her knitting, a gentle smile on her. "It's not a pretty tale," he said.

"Maybe not, but it's a true one, sir," Exe assured him. "They knew how to deal with competition in those days, wouldn't you say?"

"Is that trap thing still there?"

"No. It's all rotted away. I have to keep that part of the castle boarded up so that people can't stray up there and fall."

"And the hole—the one that went down to the dungeons?"

Mrs. Exe looked across at him, her faded eyes full of mischief. "I assure you, Mr. Donaldson, nowadays we don't put bodies down there more than once a month," she said archly.

Chapter Ten

By late evening the storm had died away, the sky clearing to display a brilliant pattern of stars undimmed by moonlight. Jay took a turn up and down in front of the dark mass of the building, sniffing appreciatively at the air fragrant with the scent of peat and damp gorse.

He looked at the luminous dial of his wrist-watch; it was almost time for Selina to be taking over a spell of duty in the bar. Five minutes later he went into the castle and was just crossing the entrance-hall when Exe called out to him.

"Mr. Donaldson. Just a moment, sir!"

The bearded man was behind the reception desk and Jay crossed over to him. "Anything wrong?"

"Good lord no, sir!" Exe smiled with a flash of white teeth in the darkness of his beard. "Should there be? . . . No, it's just something I thought might interest you." He opened a drawer in the desk and took out what looked like a postcard, for the American to see. "Would you like to sign this, sir?"

Jay picked up the object. It was a piece of thick card, with printing on it, that had been filched by Willie earlier in the day when he was on his shopping trip.

The top line read: *I am staying at*. Underneath this there was a coloured frame containing the words: *The Monsters of the Glen, at Aarolie*—these words were die-stamped and standing proud on a specially coloured piece of paper stuck on to the backing. The last two lines of print read: *The fishing is marvellous. Wish you were here*, followed by a row of dots for the signature.

"I thought there might be someone you'd like to send

it to, sir." Hogan grinned. "Publicity. You know. . . . I've been waiting to get some of these from the printer. You sign, we pay the postage. Got to build up a clientele somehow."

Jay hesitated for a moment. There wasn't a solitary person he knew in Britain. But there was a likely one back home. He took out his pen, altered the last line so that it read "Glad you are not here," and signed it after addressing it to the man to whom he had sold his business.

"Thank you, sir. I'll put a stamp on it if you'll leave it with me."

Hogan smilingly watched Jay go through the doorway that led to the bar, then turned his attenion to the postcard. He took it through into the kitchen, holding it in the steam from a kettle on the range. A moment later he peeled off the coloured patch that bore the words: *The Monsters of the Glen, at Aarolie.*

Now the opening words on the card read:

I am staying at The MacIntyre Arms, MacIntyre. The fishing is marvellous. . . .

If, after Jay Donaldson retired from the world, so to speak, anyone made inquiries . . . ! The card would be posted three or four days after the American had ostensibly left Aarolie. Hogan smiled gently to himself. There was nothing like covering one's tracks. Do that, and you couldn't go wrong.

He went and locked the card away in his desk before going through to the bar. The American was sitting perched on the far stool, talking with Selina, both enjoying some private joke, for she seemed animated enough. But when she saw Exe she drew back, becoming reserved again, and Jay flashed a puzzled look at the newcomer.

It almost seemed as though the girl was afraid of her uncle. But Exe was a pleasant enough man, despite his odd habit of bursting into booming laughter when there didn't seem to be anything funny.

"Ask your Uncle what he'll have to drink."

"Yes, sir." She did as she was told, serving the whisky efficiently enough, but as though she was—apprehensive. Only two other guests were in the bar and it didn't look as though they would be there long, for one of them was yawning and stretching as though ready to go up to bed at any moment.

Hogan eased himself on to the stool next to Jay, raising his glass in salutation. "Long life!" Three-quarters of the liquid disappeared in one swallow. "Going to try your luck with the monsters to-morrow?"

"Will it be any use?"

"Oh, the loch'll be all right, I'd say."

"Then I'll try it."

"Good. . . . Selina, give Mr. Donaldson another drink."

"I won't have another, if you don't mind. I've had my quota for the day."

Exe eyed him sardonically. "Keep fit, and all that?"

"Something like that."

"It's not a policy that appeals to me, I'm afraid. I think I've told you before. 'Take what you can, while you can.' That's my motto. You never know if you're going to see to-morrow's dawn." He tossed back the rest of the contents of his glass. "I hope you won't refuse to try my 'special' when I get some more."

"Special?"

Hogan winked. "A drop of the real stuff. Hundred per cent. proof. Makes you sleep like a baby."

"I don't think I could resist trying that."

"I'd be very hurt if you did, sir. Very hurt. . . . I'd insist on your trying it."

Jay laughed. "I wouldn't hurt you for the world, Mr. Exe."

"Good." Hogan stood up. "Well, if you'll excuse me, I'd better go the rounds to see if everyone's comfortable."

He walked out of the bar, along the passage and through the doorway into the entrance-hall. Coming towards him

112

from the other side, was Mrs. Exe. She had her head bent and was muttering to herself and as she almost bumped into him she looked up and gave a little scream.

"Hoagy! You frightened me out of my wits."

"Sorry, Mother." He made to pass, but she clutched his arm, looking round furtively to make sure they were alone.

"Wire! "

"I beg your pardon?"

"That Willie! "

Exe sighed. "What's he done now?" he asked resignedly. But instead of answering him Mrs. Exe turned and went back the way she had come, beckoning him to follow her. She led the way down into the dungeons until she came to the one where the ramp, the pile of small rocks and the wire coffin-shaped cages were stacked.

On a small table in one corner the drum of wire that Willie had brought back was standing. Mrs. Exe went up to it and held out the loose end of wire for Hogan's inspection. "Look at it."

He took it in his fingers, testing it. "It's not the right gauge."

"Exactly. Much too thin. You wouldn't be able to keep a bat inside this."

"Have you asked him about it?"

"Yes. He said he didn't notice." She shook her head sadly. "Sometimes, Hoagy, I worry about that boy. He hasn't got an ounce of brains in his head."

"Oh, Ma! "

"It's a fact. He takes after his mother. I warned you! I told you she wasn't worth having! "

"Don't let's go into that again, Ma," he said wearily.

"He'll have to take it back and change it for the right sort."

"Couldn't you use this double?"

"Waste all that money! Not likely." Mrs. Exe was shocked to think of such a suggestion coming from her son.

113

"Hoagy, I'm surprised at you."

"It was only an idea."

"Well, think again, son." She brightened. "You haven't cashed Mr. White's last pension cheque yet, have you?"

"No. . . . All right, I'll see to it to-morrow and I'll change the wire."

"I suppose it'll be safe to cash it in MacIntyre?"

"Of course. I haven't cashed one there before."

"Good. That's settled then." She stared up at him fondly. "You know I like to get ahead with my work. It takes at least a couple of days to weave one of the cages and I like to have a good stock in. I hate to run short."

"I'll see you have the stuff by to-morrow afternoon, Mother."

"That's my boy!"

Hogan watched her leave. At the doorway she turned and waved him good-bye, leaving him alone, staring into space. He stroked his beard, wondering what to do and then made up his mind. He would have a chat with the permanent guest.

White was pathetically glad to have company, even that of Exe, whose conversation at times became a rambling monologue. "Hello, Mr. Exe." Even though it was almost impossible to prevent himself from babbling—anything, so long as he was talking to *someone*, he waited. If he said the wrong thing Exe would go away. This time it was all right; Exe was in a good mood.

"You're quite comfortable, Mr. White? Being looked after properly, eh?"

"No complaints," White said hurriedly, "no complaints."

"Yes, well, nice and dry in here, isn't it? I mean, that storm this afternoon! Lucky you weren't out in it, I can tell you. Dreadful!"

Hogan perched himself comfortably on the edge of the desk and regarded the prisoner affably. "Tell me, what have you been doing with yourself all day?"

114

White couldn't restrain himself any longer. "I've been playing tennis! " he shouted. "Tennis! " His voice cracked, the second syllable rising to a shriek. Then he began to cry, sobbing quietly.

"You'll have to watch yourself, my dear fellow! " Exe said seriously. "It's not good to keep yourself apart, withdrawn. . . . You should take an interest in things."

"I want to die."

"But *I* don't want you to, Mr. White. I'm only anxious that you should live to a ripe old age." He stared round the shadowy dungeon, ignoring the sobbing man. "Yes, I suppose it is a bit quiet down here. . . . Tell me, how would you like a companion?"

The noise of the crying ceased. White's tear-stained face was turned to the bearded man, a variety of emotions changing his expression. "A—a companion?" The whisper echoed eerily through the darkness that surrounded them.

"I've been thinking about it. Trouble is, it's not easy to find the right type of guest."

"You'd bring someone else down here? Some poor unfortunate soul . . . ? I'd rather die than see that."

"I'm sure you'd like someone to talk to."

"No. If—if I could just have something to read."

"That's easy enough. If you want me to get you some books, or magazines, all you have to do is give me the money and I'll get you some."

"You know I haven't got any money! " White shouted. "Every penny, every farthing. . . . You've taken it all."

Hogan stood up, looking down at the cadaverous figure disapprovingly. "That's the trouble with the world to-day. Everyone wants everything for nothing. . . . If you can't afford a thing, then do without. I've had to go without things all my life because I couldn't afford 'em."

The harsh reproof in his voice died. When he spoke again it was as though he was explaining to a child. "Don't you see, man, if I'd been given a chance . . . ? But I never was. Oh, *They saw to that all right.* . . . But one day I'm going to tell mankind. I'm going to gain the ear of all men, to explain, to tell them. . . . Yes, if I can tell them . . . There wouldn't be any capitalists left.

"I'd take every penny they had, take it off them, see." He was beginning to get excited, his eyes blazing. "Don't you see, man?"

The deep voice began to boom, the words getting more and more difficult to understand as he strode up and down working himself into a frenzy.

White turned his face away and closed his eyes, trying to insulate himself from the man and the din of his shouting. He had heard it all a hundred, a thousand times.

Willie vaulted up on to the top bunk, adjusted his sailor hat, and lay back, reaching for the mechanism overhead. Carefully he manœuvred it until part of it stuck out through the open window behind his head.

"Up periscope!"

Outside, as he turned the handwheel to operate it, the thin stalk of metal rose steadily. Willie, his eye jammed against the viewfinder shield, saw the darkness fade, and then he was peering in at Selina's window, over the top of the curtain.

It was a very disappointing sight. She was sitting at the dressing-table, fully clothed, writing in her diary, pausing now and again as she pondered what to put down.

So far she had written:

Wonderful day, but I have been too extravagant, a new dress, when I . . .

Thoughtfully she dipped her pen in the bottle of ink and began to write again:

I don't care, it was worth it . . . and who knows . . . ?

She put the pen down, blotted the words dry, then put

the cap on the bottle of ink, as she considered what she had written.

In the wardrobe was the new dress. It was a wonderful thing, a model. The owner of the gown shop had let her have it for three-quarters of the price because it was such a small fitting, she didn't think she would be able to sell it to anyone else; even so, it was far too expensive. Getting up, Selina crossed to the wardrobe and took the garment out. Standing where she could best see her reflection in the mirror, she held the dress against her body, twisting and posturing to see it from all angles. It was the most delicious shade of blue chiffon, draped and moulded with infinite skill. She resisted the temptation to try it on, putting it back reluctantly. For a moment she saw herself as she really was and pulled a face at her reflection before starting to undress.

Willie, on his bunk in the room below, licked his lips. He made a fine adjustment to the eyepiece.

"Target coming into view, Admiral," he said hoarsely.

Ten minutes later Selina climbed into bed, gave one last loving look in the direction of the wardrobe, then reached out a hand to switch off the light.

As the eyepiece went dark, Willie suspended operations, winding the periscope down and bringing the apparatus into the room. He was restless, wondering what to do next. He prowled round the room, unable to find inspiration, then went out into the corridor, making his way towards the American's room. He looked for a light under the door, but the room was in darkness, and after listening for a moment he went downstairs, to his father's office.

In a corner of the room there was a coat rack, where Hogan kept his outdoor things. Hidden behind the folds of a tweed overcoat and a macintosh there was a stout walking stick. Cautiously, Willie removed the stick and took it over to the desk.

But the thing was not what it appeared to be, for inside

the hollow wooden stick was a rifle barrel. The thick handle
concealed the firing mechanism and Willie set the butt to
his shoulder, taking aim at the various fish in their cases
on the walls.

Next he unscrewed the end piece, leaving the muzzle
exposed, and drew from the hollowed-out wood a miniature
telescopic sight, which he fitted in place. The stick was in
fact a poacher's single-shot gun, capable of firing a .285
bullet that could kill a deer at a thousand yards.

It was not much fun, merely pointing the gun and he soon
tired of it. He put it back as he found it and left the
office. Maybe he'd take a drive. He let himself out on to
the forecourt, listening. Everything was quiet and he began
to shamble towards the lean-to. He had almost reached the
doors when someone spoke:

"Going for a run, Willie?"

It was the American, who stepped from the shadows of
the castle wall, less than a yard away. For a moment Willie's
eyes rolled wildly as he struggled to recover from the shock.
"A—a run?"

Donaldson moved closer. The more he saw of the youth
the less he liked him. "You wouldn't be thinking of borrow-
ing my car, would you?" He'd been right. The way Willie
flinched made it obvious that he was the one who had taken
the Bentley out the previous night.

"Ta—take your car, Admiral?" Willie's face was ghastly
as he strove to smile innocently.

Jay's tone was even, without emphasis, and all the more
impressive because of it. "Listen, Willie, I'll just give you
a word of warning. If I find you've been in my car again,
you'll regret it. Understand? Really regret it." He stared
hard at Willie for a moment, then turned and went towards
the entrance to the castle. He smiled briefly. The hulking
youth wouldn't do it again, he was fairly certain of that.

Willie glared after the American, as Jay's back faded into
the surrounding darkness. For a moment he raised his fist

and shook it, then changed the gesture and jerked two upright fingers into the air, putting his tongue out at the same time.

But despite his aggressive attitude, Willie thought it would be wise to be discreet. The Yankee might be hidden in the shadows, watching. Scowling, kicking at the gravel, he moved away from the lean-to.

"One day soon," he promised himself aloud, "one day soon, I'll tear your guts out, Skipper."

Chapter Eleven

JAY had only been in his room a minute when someone tapped on the door. Was it Willie, come to try to make some sort of excuse, or apology? But when he called out: "Come in," it was Hogan who entered.

"Kick me out if I'm being a nuisance, Mr. Donaldson," Exe said. "But if you've no objection I'd like to have a word with you."

"About Willie?"

Hogan looked surprised. "Why, no."

"O.K. So long as it doesn't take too long." Jay took off his jacket and loosened his tie.

"I hope we're making you comfortable, sir?"

Jay halted his movements and stared at the big man. "You didn't come to ask me that!"

"Well, no, sir." Hogan studied the contents of the room. "You're going fishing in the morning?"

"Of course. If you say the water'll be all right?"

"I'm sure it will, sir."

"Then in that case—I'm going fishing."

"I'm sorry I shan't be able to come with you—I've got one or two errands to run. . . . You know . . . essential supplies."

Jay stripped off his shirt and donned a silk dressing-gown. What in hell was Exe up to? Was he going to try to raise a loan to buy the groceries? "Well?"

Hogan made a show of dropping subterfuge. "I'll come straight to the point, Mr. Donaldson. You like the hotel, you say. And you must like the fishing also?"

"I've no complaints." Jay's tone was harsher. He was getting a little tired of Exe's presence.

"Well, sir, I can say in return I—we—we like having you here. Nothing would suit us better than to have you as a permanent guest."

"What?" Jay laughed. "Not a hope in hell, man! I'm only here for a vacation."

"I realize that. What I'm trying to say is . . . Would you care to buy the fishing rights on a stretch of water?" He went on hurriedly. "I mean, now you've been here once, I'm sure you'd come again for the fishing."

"Most likely I will, but——"

"I'm only asking you to think about it, sir," Exe went on swiftly. "Your own private piece of water where you'd be undisturbed."

Such an idea had never occurred to Jay, but now the question had been raised, it wasn't altogether displeasing. "You've done this before?"

"With quite a number of gentlemen."

Was Exe taking him to be the rich and gullible American, ready to be fleeced? "How much would it cost?"

For a moment Hogan hesitated, as though wondering what figure to quote. Then he smiled. "It isn't cheap."

"I didn't expect it would be."

"But on the other hand, it can't be too dear. I've not had any complaints from the gentlemen concerned." His smile widened. "Not a single complaint."

For the moment, Jay had had enough. "Tell me what figure you have in mind, Mr. Exe, and I'll sleep on it."

"Very well, sir. But before I do that, there is just one point. . . . I don't know how familiar you are with British income tax, Mr. Donaldson, but it's very heavy, believe me."

The American took the point immediately. "A cash deal?"

"That's the usual thing."

"Go on."

"Shall we say—ten thousand dollars?"

121

Jay laughed scornfully. *"You* can say what you like, Mr. Exe. All I'm going to say right now is: Good night!"

Later, in the four-poster, Jay thought it over; staring blindly up at the thick, padded cover above him, until he dismissed it from his mind and reached out for the book he was halfway through.

.   .   .   .   .

Hogan started out early next morning, before any of the guests were stirring. It promised to be a warm and sunny day and he listened with great patience and good humour as his Mother told him exactly what she wanted him to do in the way of shopping.

"Very well, Mother," he said finally. "I'll see there's no mistake."

"You've got Mr. White's pension thing?"

He patted his inside breast pocket. "Yes."

"And you've got the wire?"

"It's in the back," he said gently.

Mrs. Exe peered into the shooting-brake. The coil of wire that her son was to exchange lay on the floor of the vehicle. "That's a good boy!" She stooped down to peck him on the cheek. "Be careful how you drive."

"Yes, Mother."

"Some drivers are a menace."

"I'll remember that, Mother." He started the engine and put the car in gear. "Good-bye."

"Take care of yourself, son!" She stood, waving him out of sight, then went indoors to see to the guests' breakfast. Selina was bustling round, clearing the cereal plates, and Mrs. Exe took a peep through the serving hatch to see how the American looked this morning.

Donaldson was just finishing his cornflakes and she studied him for a moment, then went out into the dining-room to have a word with him.

"Good morning, Mr. Donaldson."

" 'Morning, Mrs. Exe."

122

"You'll be going out fishing today?"

"Your son said the water would be all right."

She beamed down at him. "You can trust Hogan. He's *always* right."

"Then I'd better go try my luck, hadn't I?"

"Yes. And I'll tell you a secret, Mr. Donaldson." She bent to whisper. "I think you'll have a splendid day! ... I think the fish won't be able to resist you!"

He smiled. "I hope you're right."

"I feel it in my bones. . . . Do you ever feel things in your bones, Mr. Donaldson?"

It was difficult to keep from laughing, she seemed so earnest. "Not my bones, my muscles, maybe, Mrs. Exe."

She straightened. "Oh, well, there's plenty of time yet for that sort of thing."

He watched her moving away, shaking his head, and with a puzzled smile as Selina came up to take away his cereal plate. "Your Aunt's a real character."

"Yes, sir." Her face was expressionless. "Will you have bacon and eggs, sir?"

He could have put her across his knee and dealt with her in the appropriate manner, for acting that way. But instead he ignored it. If things didn't improve tomorrow night, though, when he took her to the dance . . . ! "Yes, please," he answered solemnly. "Eggs and bacon."

When he'd finished breakfast he took his gear and a packaged lunch down to the loch-side where the rowing-boats were tied up. He took one and began to row across the water, looking up at the bright sky with some doubts. Despite what Mrs. Exe had promised him, the conditions didn't look too good.

Hogan drove into MacIntyre and was surprised to find the place full of vehicles that didn't belong to the usual holiday-makers. He manœuvred the shooting-brake into a space on the parking ground, watched by a small, red-faced attendant.

"You're very busy."

The man nodded slowly, considering how to frame his answer. "You'll be one of them?"

"One of who?"

"You'll no' be here because of the sale?"

"What sale?" Hogan had no objection to picking up a bargain.

"Up at the Museum."

Hogan grunted. He knew all about the so-called MacIntyre Museum. The family who owned it ran an antiques sale once every two or three years. It was a famous occasion, with dealers coming from all over the world to see what was offered. It was rumoured that some of the works of art "discovered" by the brothers who ran the Museum had in fact been manufactured by them.

He was annoyed that he hadn't realized that the town would be so crowded, but perhaps it was as well. There would be all that less chance of discovery if anything went wrong over the cashing of Charles White's pension cheque.

But the transaction was made without the slightest bother. The bank clerk who dealt with it asked if he was in MacIntyre for the sale, but the question was asked without any real desire to know or even have an answer.

Hogan pocketed the wad of fivers and strode out into the street looking for the nearest bar where he could wash away the remains of the strain that always tortured him at such times. By the time he'd taken his fourth double whisky he was feeling much better; he ambled out and up and down the main street, stopping to look at the posters announcing the auction.

Jay tried his first cast from the boat, more as an experiment than anything else, and when the fly was taken he was almost unprepared. Whatever was on the other end of the line must have been about the size of a young whale, for the

124

nylon snapped as though it was a strand of cotton, and the boat lurched so viciously that he nearly went into the water.

But that seemed likely to be the one and only bit of excitement. During the next few hours he tried every trick he knew, without getting even a suspicion of a bite. Neither from the boat nor the land did he have the smallest indication of success and by the time he ate his cold lunch he was wondering whether to quit for the day and return to the castle.

The granite-grey mass of the building loomed on the far side of the loch and as he chewed on the leg of a chicken he wondered how it must have looked to would-be invaders. He shivered suddenly as a gust of wind struck his back, and he turned his head to survey the weather. The sky was clouding over; at the other end of the glen grey masses were piling up and the freshly risen wind was driving them down towards where he was sitting.

Jay looked at the sky calculatingly. If there was going to be a return visit from the storm, he didn't wish to be caught in it. But from the look of the clouds he'd have a bit more time to try to kill a fish, although it seemed barely worth while attempting it. What he had earlier assumed to be a bite had probably been a sunken log or branch brought down into the loch by a fast-moving mountain stream.

He stared up at the sky again, then at his luminous wrist watch, making a calculation. Thirty minutes. He'd give himself another thirty minutes before starting to row back.

As he resumed casting, he found that it was not only the weather that had changed; his luck had also altered. A fish rose not twenty feet in front of the spot where his fly had landed. He followed the line of rises, gauging exactly where he would have to put his fly at the next cast.

He did it perfectly, thrilling with pleasure at the skill he managed. If he'd been casting over land the fly would have dropped on a dime. But then the fish rose again and he knew he'd got it firmly hooked. Its size, when he netted it, would have seemed gigantic to any average trout fisherman, but it was far from being a monster.

Now that he'd killed a fish he would have to try for another. The wind was freshening, rippling the surface of the water farther out from the shore. It was almost time to go, but he couldn't leave the spot, not now. Not until he'd tried once more.

This time he didn't have to wait. Scarcely able to believe his luck, within seconds of casting the fly had been taken—and by something huge. Whatever he'd got, it certainly wasn't a sunken, waterlogged piece of timber, for from the moment he struck, Jay had a fight on his hands, and with the passing of minutes it grew fiercer.

It was exhilarating, his whole body responding to the thrill of it as he fought his catch. "Come on, you beauty!" he breathed aloud, as he kept up the strain, trying to sense what the fish would do next and to avoid putting extra tension on the line for it was almost at breaking-point a dozen, a score of times as the fish fought to break free.

When it leapt from the water, showing all its huge bulk, his heart seemed to leap in unison. The trout was truly one of the monsters and he didn't dare to estimate its weight. It was tiring now, but this didn't make the battle any easier for Jay's strength was waning too, sapped by the struggle.

Then came the moment when he had it in to the bank. Landing it was about the most difficult physical task he'd ever attempted and he knew with sick certainty that he'd never be able to achieve it. He was lying face down, the rod in his left hand, net in the right hand and trying hopelessly to manipulate the two, when he heard a deep voice behind him.

"You'll have taken a fish, Mr. Donaldson?"

Jay twisted his neck for a moment to look who was speaking. It was Tam Bruce, uniformed and incongruously clutching the handles of his bicycle. "Help me with the net!" Jay gasped.

Tam did as he was asked, but not willingly. Trout, he supposed, were all very well, but there was only one fish—the salmon. Anything else was not worthy of the name. It took him a second to slip the net under the beastie and lift it from the water.

"Did you ever see anything like *that*!" Jay made no effort to get up, but lay there peering at the monstrous trout with delight. Almost certainly it would tip the scales at over twenty pounds. As he gazed at it he remembered Mrs. Exe's remarks. Yes, he'd surely had a fine bit of sport. Slowly he got up.

"Thanks, Mr. Bruce. I don't think I'd have got him without your help."

"You'll be going back to Aarolie, sir?"

"Yes." Jay looked up at the sky. During the time he'd spent fighting the trout the clouds had thickened until they were solid. "Yes, right away, I think."

"Aye, we're going to have a wee bit wet." Bruce coughed. "You'd be kind enough to give me and ma machine a lift across the water, Mr. Donaldson?"

"Of course." Jay was packing his gear and trying not to spend too much time staring at his huge catch. "You've been chasing poachers?"

The policeman took the question seriously. "Aye, in a manner of speaking, sir."

They were standing on a level shelf of rock. Behind them the granite rose, making it impossible to see more than twenty yards from the water's edge. Bruce must have come down the gulley that led crosswise on to the level shelf. Jay pointed to the cleft. "You came down there?"

It was a daft question, Tam considered, but didn't say so. Did the American foreigner think that he had flown to the spot on his bicycle? "Aye, sir. 'Tis the only way unless you can climb."

"Is it far from the road?" Jay wasn't really interested. He was asking the questions in order to prevent himself from gloating and boasting over his catch.

"Three, four miles."

All the gear was packed now and Jay climbed into the boat, taking the various packages as Tam handed them down. Then came the bicycle and the policeman held it in position, balanced across the thwarts, as the American got out the oars.

They reached the other side before the rain began and Jay was just getting his gear out of the boat, after unloading the policeman's bicycle, as the first drops spattered down.

With the boat safely tied up and Tam escorting him, the American began to hurry towards the entrance. As he did so he saw the Exes' shooting-brake coming up the drive, Hogan at the wheel. The bearded man was in a pleasant frame of mind, calling out a greeting as he stopped the vehicle near the post that supported the inn sign.

"A good day's sport, Mr. Donaldson? . . .

Jay held up his trophy and Hogan smiled with pleasure. "Splendid! You're getting into the way of it, eh?" He turned to the solemn-faced policeman. "Did you help Mr. Donaldson to arrest it, Tam?" Exe got out of the brake, without waiting to hear Bruce's reply. "Is it the right time of day to drink to the catch, do you think?" The question was addressed only to Bruce; Jay had gone ahead, out of the rain.

"I'm on duty, Mr. Exe."

"Of course you are, Tam. You're never off it, are you! . . . But it's going to rain and you'll be soaked by the time you get home. So I'm going to insist you have a drop for medicinal reasons."

"That's verra guid of you, sir."

"Mr. Donaldson's waiting for us to weigh his trout." Head bent against the increasingly heavy rain, Exe hurried inside, Tam followed at a more sedate pace, in deference to his official status. The shooting-brake was loaded with various stores and, almost hidden by the other items, a reel of wire. There must be a gey amount of fence repairing for the castle proprietors to do.

The trout weighed an ounce and a half short of twenty-four pounds and it was duly celebrated. Even Selina looked pleased, although she admitted to Jay that she found it difficult to work up a great deal of enthusiasm over a dead fish.

"Or even a live fish, come to that," she said with an uncharacteristic show of spirit.

Jay remembered just how alive the fish had been, when it was a trial of strength between the two of them—that was the thrilling part of it. Now it was dead, he supposed it wasn't very important to him. He was propping up the bar with his elbows, watching Selina tolerantly as she poured a double tot of rum for Mrs. Exe who had popped into the small room. This evening the old woman was dressed in swathing white robes and a flowing headdress; she said it was the costume of a Druid priestess.

"Of course," she admitted to the American, "this isn't a genuine *costume,* although the detail is accurate."

"I can see it is," Jay agreed solemnly. The old girl looked like a refugee from a Hallowe'en party.

"I made it myself." She turned to take the glass from Selina and tipped half the contents down her throat with a smooth, practised motion.

"It must have been very difficult for a Druid, Mr. Donaldson, I mean . . . waiting for the Summer Solstice, in this climate. . . . I ask you! " She emptied the glass, put it down and said, to no one in particular: "Supper! "

Jay grinned, winking at Selina. The old girl must have meant that the rum was her supper, for it was almost time for the bar to close; dinner had been finished hours before. Mrs. Exe peered into her glass to make certain it was empty, then made an exit, draperies swirling.

"Has she always been like that?"

Selina nodded. "As long as I can remember."

But he wasn't really very interested in the grandmother. "Looking forward to tomorrow?"

"Why should I be?"

Her rather sad blue eyes were regarding him calmly, not giving any indication if she was joking and for a moment he felt uncomfortable under their scrutiny. Selina was beautiful, but there was a quality about her that he couldn't quite define and sometimes it made him wonder about her. There was an ice-wall of reserve around her that he wanted to melt. Was it the so-called British phlegm? Or was it something more than that?

"How about giving me a preview of your ball-gown?" The words were lightly spoken and they obviously appealed to her, for she laughed.

"It's nothing as grand as that!"

"O.K., then, so it's a dress. Do I get to see it?"

"Tomorrow, yes." She gave him a dreamy sort of smile.

Thinking about the dress filled her with a warm sense of pleasure. It had been too long since she had treated herself to anything so lovely, and she could hardly wait to go up to her room so that she could look at it again.

It was another hour before she could get away and when she got to her bedroom and switched on the light she hurried straight to her wardrobe, keenly anticipating the thrill of seeing the dress and holding it against her—no, this time she would put it on, she wanted to make sure now that it looked as wonderful on her as it had in the shop.

"Oh, dear!"

The blue dress had slipped from its hanger and was lying crumpled at the bottom of the wardrobe. She lifted it carefully, it was such luxurious material that it wouldn't crease easily, but the sight of it like that was distressing. She held it up and shook it, enjoying the feel of it. Would the American approve? He had told her to get blue, and this, surely, must be the most glorious shade that even he had ever seen.

She carried it across to the bed and laid it down ready to slip on, then gave a sudden cry of horror. The back of it was marked with a huge black stain. She ran back and looked wildly into the wardrobe to see what could have done the damage.

In the bottom of the wardrobe, under the empty hanger, was her ink-bottle, cork out and on its side.

Chapter Twelve

JAY let himself into the castle and made for the staircase. It was late, past midnight, and the hall was deserted and silent. But as he reached the top of the stairs he imagined he heard a sound that made him halt, listening. Yes, there it was again; the muffled noise of a woman crying.

So far as he could tell the sound came from somewhere along the corridor to his right—not too far from the first room he had occupied. It was a weird experience; was he about to see a ghost? Anything was possible in such a setting, but after a moment he shrugged off the idea. Those sobs were a living woman's and they must almost certainly be Selina's.

He moved along the corridor and round a corner. The sounds were louder and now he could guess where they were coming from. Ahead and on the right a door was ajar, light streaming from the opening into the dimly lit passage. He recognized the door as being the one that gave access to the bathroom.

Outside the door he paused. "That you, Selina?" The sobs were immediately stifled, but there was no reply. Sure now that something was wrong, he pushed open the door. Selina, her face wet with tears, was staring at him miserably. She had some blue thing she was washing in the handbasin and as he went in to her he saw she had been scrubbing part of what appeared to be a dress.

"Honey, what's wrong?"

"I—I—there's been an accident." Her voice was so shuddery with sobs, he could hardly make out the words.

"You're hurt?"

"My—my dress." Helplessly she held it out for his

132

inspection and he saw a great wet patch in the material, with a darker stain in the middle of it.

"This is your new dress?"

"Yes."

It looked like a piece of old rag. "What happened?"

From the way she hesitated, gulping, it was obvious that she wasn't going to tell the truth. "What happened?" he said again.

"I—there was some ink spilt on it."

He took out a handkerchief from his breast pocket and offered it to her; but she shook her head, fumbling for her own. "Is that the dress you bought for the dance?" She nodded dumbly and he regarded her carefully. What he was going to suggest would need tact. "It's the only one you have?"

"Yes."

Jay put out a hand and held her gently by her forearm. "There's no chance of getting another?"

"Of course not." She pulled her arm free. "It serves me right. I should never have bought it."

"How did it happen?" She seemed oddly reluctant to tell him. "I want to know Selina. . . . Was it Willie?"

She caught her breath, moving back from him sharply and staring with frightened eyes. "No! " she gasped. "No! "

It was all too obvious that the youth was the culprit. Jay felt himself flush with anger, but he managed to speak gently, so as not to alarm the girl who looked almost ready to collapse from weariness and misery.

"Show me how it happened." He took the ruined dress from her trembling fingers and after a moment's hesitation she did as she was told, leading him out and to the narrow spiral stair that led to the floor above.

When she reached her bedroom Jay was a pace or two behind her. With one hand on the door-knob she hesitated, looking back at him, then opened the door. Across the room, peering in at her through the window was an enormous skull-like monstrosity. The shock of it was finally too much. With a little moaning scream she crumpled in a faint, Jay leaping forward too late to catch her.

He knelt beside her, then looked round in bewilderment, trying to make out what had scared her. Apart from the fact that the curtains were not drawn, everything seemed normal. He picked her up and carried her to the bed, chafing her wrists briskly and bending anxiously over her.

"Selina! Are you all right?"

Gradually she regained consciousness, then sat up jerkily, staring wide-eyed and shuddering at the window. "Did you see it?" she whispered.

"See what?"

"That—that thing at the window."

He went over to look out but there was only darkness, with not even the gleam of a single star to lighten the sky. He drew the curtains and went back to the bed. "There's nothing there."

"When I went out the curtains were drawn."

She was nervously pushing her long blonde hair back from her face and he saw the still-visible marks across the backs of the fingers of her right hand.

"What was it you saw?"

"Please! "

But he wasn't going to be put off. "What was it, Selina?"

"A—a face." It made her shudder to think of it.

He stared round the room, then went across to the wardrobe, opening the door. It was immediately obvious where the ink had been spilt and he looked at her. "Where do you usually keep your ink?"

Wordlessly she pointed to the dressing-table. There was a pen and an empty ink-bottle resting on a piece of blotting-paper.

"Where does Willie sleep?"

The question surprised her. She swung her feet to the floor and stared across at him. The expression on his face was one she hadn't seen before, grim and boding ill for someone. "Please, I don't want any trouble."

"Where's his room?"

"Underneath this one."

He nodded. Everything was clear to him now. Willie must have seen the girl leave the room and go down to try to wash the stain from her dress. He must have gone into her bedroom, opened the curtains and then probably gone back to his own place to fix a mask on a stick or something to wave outside her window.

She was very close now, looking up at him appealingly. "Please. I don't want any trouble. Don't tell my Uncle."

Jay put his hands on her shoulders. "I won't. . . . Listen. The only trouble is going to be for Willie. And that's a promise. I'll see to it that he drops these charming little tricks. Understand? It'll be O.K. from now on. . . . And don't worry about the dance. I reckon your Aunt'll be able to lend you something. After all, you can wear fancy dress if you like. You'd look great as a Druid priestess."

Selina giggled rather shakily. The presence of the big American was comforting. If only she could confide in him . . . but she was too weary.

"Sleep well. Leave everything to me." He put one hand under her chin lifting her tear-stained face and patting her on the tip of her nose with an affectionate forefinger. "Sleep well, sweetheart."

He turned and smiled at her before closing the bedroom door, but then, out in the corridor, his expression changed to one of fury. He raced down the spiral stairs three at a time and stormed along to the corresponding door on the lower corridor.

"Open up, Willie!"

There might be other people in the adjacent rooms, but he didn't give a damn. He hammered on the door with a clenched fist. "Come on, blast you, open up or I'll kick the door in! "

A moment later the door was thrown open and Willie, with one of his sailor caps perched on the back of his head, stood grinning at him. "Something wrong, Captain?"

Jay put one hand against the big youth's chest and pushed with all his force, sending the young man reeling back into the room. Willie was still grinning foolishly as Jay followed him into the room and closed the door. Some of the smile faded when Donaldson turned the key in the lock and put the key in his pocket.

"Here, this is my cabin——"

"Listen to me, Willie." Jay was keeping tight control over his anger. "If you play one single trick more on your cousin, I'll break every bone in your body."

"You an' who else!" Willie's confidence was returning. He moved forward until he was almost touching the American. "Listen, if I tell my Dad you'ce been messing about in her room——"

He got no further. A flash of rage made Jay grip the youth's clothing, pulling him forward until their faces were inches apart. "One more filthy suggestion out of you, young Willie . . ." He shook the young man viciously, making his head snap backwards and forwards, and then threw him off in revulsion. Willie staggered, tripping and falling back heavily, hitting his head against the wall.

"Do you get the message, Willie?" Jay stood looming over the supine, blubbering youth. He clenched a fist, holding it in front of the other's face and shaking it menacingly. "Do you?"

"I won't do nothing again, Admiral. I swear!" Willie was in a panic, trying to scramble away from the rock-like fist, but he was trapped in a corner. "I swear it on the Holy Bible!"

Jay straightened up, looking down at the repulsive creature and wondering if what he had done was sufficient to make the youth keep to his word. "O.K. But I'm going to keep an eye on you, Willie, and the first mistake you make,

I promise you . . . ! " He took the key from his pocket and unlocked the door.

Willie raised himself on one elbow and watched the American leave. The youth was sobbing, trembling from the shock and the pain of the blow against the back of his head. His tear-wet face was contorted by hate as he whispered a promise to himself.

"One day soon, Mister Yank, I'll cut your bastard heart out and feed it to the fishes myself."

Mrs. Exe bustled round the kitchen, preparing Charles White's breakfast tray. She finished spooning out his ration of porridge and turned to put the cooking pot back on the stove: Jay Donaldson was striding towards her. She pressed a hand to her bosom.

"Oh, dear! "

"I'm sorry if I scared you, Mrs. Exe." It was the last thing he wanted to do. Jay had come down specially early to have a word with the old woman, to ask a favour in fact. "Look, I hope you won't take this amiss . . . ?"

"Until I know what it is, dear boy . . . ?"

"Selina told you she's going to a dance with me this evening?"

"And a very good thing too. Enjoy yourself while you can." She nodded firmly. "That's a sound motto, Mr. Donaldson. You never know how soon the grave will claim you."

"I know you're busy, so I'll come straight to the point." It was the only way to shut the old girl up. Given half a chance, she'd go on for hours. "Selina had an accident——"

Mrs. Exe gave a piercing scream of horror. "Is she badly hurt?"

"She's not hurt at all." It was as much as he could do to keep his temper. "The accident was to her dress. It's ruined. She hasn't got anything to wear. . . . I—I thought maybe one of the costumes you have . . . ?" He broke off as Hogan came in, carrying a pile of newly split logs for the range. But Hogan dumped the wood and went out again without paying any attention to him and Jay resumed his plea:

"It's fancy dress as well. . . ."

"You mean have *I* got anything she could borrow?"

He smiled. "That's it. You know. . . ."

At any other time she would have been consumed with rage to hear such a suggestion, but Hogan wanted the American to feel at home. "Why didn't Selina come straight to me?"

"She probably will. And I hope you won't let her know I've asked you."

Mrs. Exe patted his arm. "Leave it to me."

"Thank you. I'm very grateful."

She beamed up at him. "And now, if you'll excuse me, I'm very busy." She picked up the breakfast tray as he hurried out of the kitchen, making his apologies. As he passed through the doorway he met Willie.

"Morning, Admiral. Fleet out for exercise?" Grinning, Willie strolled past Jay, the events of the night apparently forgotten. Shaking his head in wonder, Jay went outdoors for a brisk walk before breakfast.

Despite the emotional stresses of the previous evening, Selina slept well and woke later than usual. In a panic she washed and dressed hurriedly, then rushed down to the kitchen. It was empty, but preparation for breakfast was well under way and she went through into the dining-room to put out the baskets of fresh rolls. Those seen to, the next job was to serve the butter pats, and she returned to the kitchen for them.

Mrs. Exe, tray in hand, was just coming in through the doorway that led to the wine-cellars. "Ah, Selina dear, I've been looking for you."

The old lady was in her usual gentle, smiling mood and the girl took advantage of it, her words coming out with a

138

rush. "Aunty, could I borrow a costume from your collection?"

Mrs. Exe put down the tray and regarded her, frowning in apparent puzzlement. "Borrow one of my costumes, dear? Whatever for?"

"I—I spilt ink on my dress. You know I'm going to a dance tonight, with Mr. Donaldson."

"And your frock's ruined?" She made sympathetic noises. "Then we'll have to see what we can do, won't we! . . . But you'll be careful with it, won't you? I mean, they're very valuable, you know."

"Oh, Aunty!" Selina flung her arms round the plump old woman and kissed her cheek. "Thank you."

"Don't thank me. Just take care of it. . . . And of yourself. These Americans!"

"I'm sure Mr. Donaldson's all right, Aunty." The old dear wouldn't understand if she tried to explain how sure she felt about it.

"Don't you trust him an inch, my girl. Not an inch. You read some dreadful accounts in the papers about what Americans have done. They're very dangerous people. Violent."

Selina just smiled; it was no good discussing anything with her Aunt.

Although Selina had known about her Aunt's mania for period costumes, she'd never realized just how extensive the collection was. There were two wardrobes full of dresses that Mrs. Exe wore from time to time, and one cupboardful which she was working on, changing and altering the various robes and gowns until they could accommodate her ample girth.

But there was in addition another double wardrobe filled with items that Mrs. Exe could not adapt for her own use. They were male costumes that involved the use of tights. Selina lingered over her selection for a long time. There wasn't anything becoming enough in blue. Finally she chose a Robin Hood outfit in Lincoln green velvet. The costume consisted of a jaunty cap with a long, pheasant's feather, a simple jerkin tied in at the waist, and tights that would, she knew, show off her legs to perfection. She was proud of her legs, they were long and slender.

"Can I borrow this, Aunty?"

Mrs. Exe looked dubious. "Won't you be making rather a display of your limbs?" She brooded over the problem for a moment, Selina watching her anxiously, then she gave her consent. It was perhaps the least valuable of her collection and she felt grateful to the girl for choosing that particular one.

"You'd better try it on and see if it needs taking in at all."

Hogan was in what was, for him, a considerate mood. When Selina finished drying the last of the tea things, he told her to go up to her room. "Willie can see to your jobs from now on," he said. "I dare say you'd like time to make yourself pretty."

"Thank you, Uncle." It was unexpected; she'd assumed he would keep her busy until the very last moment.

"Enjoy yourself, girl." He leaned close to her. "And be nice to Donaldson," he whispered.

She looked round in surprise, then decided not to comment. From the way the words had been spoken, her Uncle might be suggesting . . . ? She was never quite sure about him. "I'm very grateful to him."

"So you should be, lass. A man like that—a millionaire, going to take *you* out . . . !" He raised his eyebrows significantly. "You never know what might happen!"

"Stop teasing her, Hogan, you naughty boy!" Mrs. Exe was regarding him sternly. She turned to Selina. "You heard your Uncle. Off with you! Go on." She waited until the girl was out of the kitchen. "You think it's all right to let her go out with that young man? Americans get up to all sorts of tricks."

Hogan stared up at the high ceiling as though looking for inspiration. "Tell you what, Ma. If we find he's been naughty, we'll put it on the bill."

"Has he said anything more?"

"I haven't seen him. He's been away all day."

At that moment, however, Jay was steering the silver-grey Bentley over the cattle grid that marked the entrance to the long drive up to the castle. When he had heard from Selina that she had borrowed a costume he had gone looking for one for himself. The choice had been very limited; he hadn't got the nerve to wear the kilt, so Bonnie Prince Charlie was out. By great good fortune there was something else that fitted—appropriately it was that of an American pioneer backwoodsman, complete with fringed buckskin and racoon cap.

Selina took a final look at herself in the bedroom mirror, then took the feathered cap off. She plaited her long hair and twisted it into a coronet so that none of it would show under the cap, then slipped an old raincoat over the Robin Hood costume. She had just tied the belt when someone knocked and Jay called out:

"Hey, there! Will you be long?"

She went to the door and opened it, staring in surprise at the buckskin jacket and the cap he held in his hand. Oddly enough she hadn't given a thought to what he would be wearing, but already one thing was certain: no other girl would have such a handsome escort.

Jay grinned. "You're not going to keep that thing on?" He pointed to her raincoat.

"Of course not!"

"Then take it off now and let me have the full effect." He watched her do as she was told. In an odd way she seemed specially defenceless dressed like that. The slender neck with the hair lifted away from it looked childish, but her legs were magnificent and she was altogether lovely. Suddenly he felt he wanted to protect her from all hurt and he suffered a moment of keen regret that he hadn't kicked Willie all round the glen when he'd had the opportunity. His thoughts must have been reflected on his face for she asked anxiously:

"Don't you like it?"

He dismissed Willie from his mind. "You look lovely, really lovely."

Selina smiled uncertainly. "Can I put my coat on again now?"

He bowed deeply before taking her coat to help her on with it. "Maid Marian, you may do as you wish." He would have to keep the conversation flippant for he had been surprised and shaken by the depth of feeling the sight of her had aroused, and he wasn't at all sure whether he cared for such emotion.

The Bentley was just outside the front entrance, parked where Jay had left it, on his return. He helped Selina in, then went round to the off-side and climbed into the driver's seat. In their trip down from Selina's bedroom they had managed to avoid meeting anyone, but as the Bentley moved off, Willie stared after it balefully. Maybe the Yank would get tight, crash the car and cause the girl and himself to be burned to death. The thought made Willie feel a little better.

Jay was steering the silver-grey car down the narrow drive and as he reached the cattle grid he came almost to a halt before turning right. As he swung out on to the road another car came into view round the bend two hundred yards to the left. Its driver pressed frantically on the horn button when he saw the Bentley, but Jay was too far away to hear.

"Damn and blast it!"

The second driver stared resentfully after the Bentley, which was accelerating away smoothly and growing smaller in the distance. His own car gave another bucking jerk, then

142

sounded as though its engine was rattling itself to pieces. The man, Gordon Creighton, pulled up at the spot from which the Bentley had emerged. There was a narrow track leading up between the trees and a telephone line that bordered the road.

A drive, a telephone, a car. That meant that this part of the infernal country *was* inhabited. Ever since he'd taken the wrong fork miles back and the engine had started to make queer noises, he'd been under the growing conviction that there was no human being other than himself in the whole of the Highlands.

It might be that the car he'd seen leave had carried away the people who lived in the house at the end of the drive he was staring at. But there might still be someone there. At least he could use the telephone . . . ? Three minutes later, as he stared up at the sign, *The Monsters of the Glen,* he congratulated himself on his good fortune. To drop on an hotel in such fashion was the luckiest break he'd had in ages.

A huge, black-bearded man was striding towards the car. "Good evening, sir."

"Good evening. I say—this *is* an hotel?"

"Yes."

"Thank the Lord for that! "

Hogan eyed the newcomer speculatively. He was a young, fussily dressed man who appeared to be under a great strain. "Your car doesn't sound too healthy."

"Have you a mechanic, a garage?"

"Nothing like that, sir. I could telephone for one, but he wouldn't get here before to-morrow morning."

"You've got a room?"

"We can fix you up all right, sir. I don't know about dinner, though. It would have to be a scratch meal."

"That'll do splendidly." Creighton sighed in relief. He went to the boot of his car and opened it. There were three pieces of luggage inside, lightweight, initialled cases. He took the smallest one out. "I'd like you to put this in the hotel safe."

Hogan tensed. "Certainly, sir." There *was* no hotel safe, but he didn't allow such small details to interfere with business. "Are the contents very valuable, sir? Just for the record," he added hastily.

Gordon Creighton drew himself up to his full height of five foot four and one-quarter inches. "As a matter of fact, landlord, they are extremely valuable. Quite a responsibility." He gave a high-pitched laugh. "I was at the MacIntyre sale, you know," he offered casually. It was the first time he had been entrusted with an expensive purchase, but he didn't intend to reveal the fact. Or that he had been the only person available, otherwise he wouldn't have been sent.

"The MacIntyre sale!" Exe sounded suitably impressed, although his mind was busy with other things. He became aware that the little man was staring up at him, impatience growing. "I'm sorry, sir, I was just working out what was best to do. We're rather short-handed at the moment—most of the staff are off to a dance. But if you'll come with me . . . ?"

He picked up the two remaining suitcases and strode quickly towards the entrance, with Creighton trotting in an effort to keep up. Whatever else had to be done, the new-comer must be kept out of sight of the other guests, for the time being at least. Hogan wasn't sure whether a fine fish had fallen into his net, but with a bit of time at his disposal he intended to find out.

Exe got to the entrance-hall and took a quick peep to ensure that it was empty. He hurried across its vast floor towards his own office. "Follow me, sir," he said to the wondering visitor. "I hope you don't mind——" The door on the far side of the hall swung open and Hogan swore. But it was his Mother, dressed in one of her costumes. She sailed through and disappeared through a further door without even seeing either of the two men.

Creighton gaped. "Who—who's that?"

"Mary Queen of Scots." Hogan glanced back. The little man looked as though he was going to run for his life. "It's all right, sir," he said smilingly. "The dance is fancy dress."

Gordon Creighton gave a sickly grin of relief. For a moment he'd thought . . . well, he didn't know what he'd thought. When the bearded man took him into an office whose walls were lined with stuffed fish in glass cases he dismissed them after one glance. Fishing was not one of his interests. In fact, Gordon had very few interests, apart from Gordon Creighton.

"Can I offer you a drink, sir?" Hogan was already pouring out a measure of whisky.

"Thank you, no. I never touch alcohol."

Exe put the decanter down thoughtfully. "You're very wise, sir. Drink can lead to all sorts of consequences." He looked gravely pensive for a moment. "I'll go and arrange a room for you, sir. Shall I take that case and lock it in the safe?" He sat down opposite the visitor and reached for pen and paper. "If you'll give me a list of the contents, I'll give you a written receipt."

It was the first reassuring thing Creighton had heard. "It's an altar chalice. Sixteenth-century Italian. Gold, with ruby and diamond encrustings."

The words were written down solemnly. "Gold, with rubies and diamonds," Exe said admiringly. "That'll be worth a packet of money, I'll be bound."

Admiration, deserved or not, was a drug Creighton couldn't resist. "I had to pay a few thousand for it."

Hogan became briskly efficient. "Then in that case the sooner I put it in the safe, the better." He went to the door, then paused. "Lucky you found the hotel, sir. Who told you about us?"

"No one. I saw a car drive out."

"A silver-grey Bentley?"

145

"I think so."

"That'd be one of our guests. A very nice gentleman. An American millionaire." He watched the other man preen himself at the thought of being in close proximity to a millionaire. "You didn't speak to him?"

"I didn't have a chance; he was too far ahead."

"Oh, well!" Hogan smiled consolingly. "Maybe you'll get to meet him in the morning." He opened the door. "And now, if you'll excuse me for a minute, sir, I'll go and see what I can arrange for you."

It took Hogan a matter of seconds to find Willie. "Job for you, son." He thrust the case at the youth. "Open that."

Willie grinned, taking a bunch of keys and picklocks from his pocket. He had made them himself and they were capable of opening any lock he had ever seen. "Dead easy." He made one testing probe, and then the case was open. Inside there was a smaller, green leather case and a small package.

The second case contained the chalice. The package contained just under seven hundred pounds in ten-pound notes, plus a receipt for four thousand, one hundred guineas, paid for the purchase of the Matalinni Chalice. Willie stared expectantly at his father. "What's all this, Dad?"

"It means we've got another customer, lad. . . . But we'll have to work fast. Where's your Granny?"

"Serving in the bar."

"Right. Tell her we've got another Club member joining. Then as soon as you've done that, get up to the 'special' room and clear everything of Donaldson's out of it. We'll want to use the room."

"Isn't it a bit risky, Dad?" Willie remembered the awful threats the American had made. "Couldn't we do it differently?"

"Son, if we're going to do a job, then that job has to be done properly, with due ceremony. It's not just any old thing, you know. It's a solemn business; we must do it respectfully."

"Yes, Dad."

"Then clear everything out of Donaldson's room, but remember where you took it from so you can put it back after."

"O.K."

"And tell your Granny she'll have to make some special soup or something. Our prospective member doesn't drink."

"O.K."

When Willie had gone off on his errand, Hogan put the case into one of the kitchen cupboards, then went back to attend to Creighton's comforts. On his way he made a slight detour to put the telephone out of action. One never knew; the man might want to phone someone.

Jay stopped the Bentley at a point where the road curved. Over to their left there was a panoramic view of the mountains forming a backcloth of green and purple to the silver river, winding far below where they were parked on a level strip of grass. Selina looked at him in surprise.

"I don't know about you," he said, "but I'm famished. I didn't have any dinner."

She was immediately guilty. "I'm sorry—I never thought . . . ." Only now did it occur to her that she hadn't had anything either since lunch-time, except a cup of tea.

He leaned over the back of his seat and threw aside the rug that hid a hamper. "I thought we'd have a snack." He opened the hamper casually, concealing the pleasure he felt from seeing the expression on her face. She was suddenly animated, watching with excited interest as he took a bundle of snowy-white paper napkins from the top of the carefully packed basket.

There was enough food for half a dozen people, starting with hot soup from a "Thermos" flask. With the barbecued chicken legs and green salad, Jay produced a bottle of champagne, getting out of the car to open it. He handed her a glass that had been carefully packed in tissue paper. "Have that ready!" The cork sailed up and into the valley, as she leaned over for the glass to be filled.

The fruit salad and fresh cream was delicious. Selina ate and drank with a hearty appetite and by the time she was sipping at the scalding coffee, she had to loosen the belt of her raincoat. "So that's what you call a snack." She laughed as she added candidly, "I don't know when I ate so much, I've been a pig."

He took her empty cup. "I like to see people enjoy their food, especially slim young blondes."

"You planned all this, didn't you?" She gestured with her hand to include the magnificent scene spread out before them.

"I figured it was a good spot to park." His gaze was focused on the distant mountains.

Selina turned to him laying her hand on his arm and looking up into his face shyly. "You're very kind," she said softly. "Kinder than . . ." She broke off and he saw the tears in her eyes before she turned away, taking her hand from his arm. "Thank you."

He started to pack the things back into the hamper.

"The evening hasn't started yet."

But as far as Gordon Creighton was concerned, the evening was almost over. The scratch meal his host had produced was excellent and the little man was feeling somewhat sleepy. But Exe seemed to want to talk, to ask more questions. Creighton supplied the answers, but he jibbed. He wanted to go to bed. Tomorrow was going to be a big day, for he had to get down to Liverpool in a hurry to hand the chalice over to an American buyer who was sailing on Monday.

He stood up. "If you'd show me to my room," he suggested.

"Certainly, sir."

148

"What about my car?"

"I've asked my son to have a look at it. He's a very good mechanic. Strictly amateur, of course, but he can usually find the cause of any trouble and put it right."

"Good." Creighton yawned. Suddenly he was most extraordinarily tired. Probably the excitement of the day and then a large meal. He followed Exe, only just conscious of the huge, deserted entrance-hall. One thing he had meant to ask was how many guests there were, but that could wait. All he wanted now was a bed. He became aware that the bearded man was gripping his arm, helping him along. At any other time he would have resented the gesture, but at the moment it was a great help.

"This is your room, sir." Exe had thrown open a door and the newcomer stared round in awed surprise. It was a grand room, fit for a nobleman. And the bed. . . . Knees buckling, he went towards the four-poster.

"I think you'll find you sleep soundly tonight, sir," Exe said, helping him to lie on top of the sheets. "I assure you it won't be my fault if you don't."

"Than' you . . . ver' kind." The words were muffled and indistinct. A moment later they were followed by a rasping snore.

Satisfied, Hogan went downstairs and took the Registration Book through to his office. The book was a loose-leaf ledger. Thoughtfully he removed the sheet that bore Creighton's signature and address, tearing it up and striking a match to the scrap paper.

Now, if the police checked, there would be no record that Creighton had ever stayed at the castle.

Chapter Thirteen

WITH every mile they drove, Selina became more and more animated. The depression that had always seemed to hover over her at the castle had gone. Jay spared a moment from time to time to glance sideways at the girl. Maybe it was the champagne she'd drunk that made her talkative, but whatever it was he didn't want to stop her.

"All right, what happened then, after your Mother died?"

"Daddy brought me back to Scotland." She turned to peer at him. "Look, I've told you all about me. What about you?"

"Nothing to tell."

She was staring at him curiously. "Is it true you're a millionaire?"

The question surprised him. "Who told you that?"

"Uncle Hogan."

The question was: who'd told Hogan? Jay hadn't mentioned his financial status. "You mustn't believe everything your Uncle tells you, Selina," he said lightly.

"Why did you come here?"

"To Aarolie?" He laughed. "A sentimental journey. I was looking for the home of my ancestors. They came from these parts." He laughed again. "You know what? I haven't even tried to track them down since I've been here."

"You mean your people came from the glen?" She was excited again. "So did mine! I've still got the old croft, on the other side of the mountains."

"Are you what they call the Laird?"

Her laughter was like music. "I'm not even a Lairdess! No, it isn't really a croft, though. More like a hill farm, and about the poorest piece of grazing in the Highlands. One

150

sheep per hundred acres."

"You own a hundred acres?"

"Three hundred. At least, I don't exactly own them. Not yet."

She was providing fresh surprises for him every minute. Three hundred acres! That was a fair piece of ground in which to put down roots. "If you've got that much land, why do you work for your Uncle?"

Some of the sparkle left her eyes. "We have an—arrangement. I work here in the summer, to keep myself alive on my farm during the winter." She smiled resignedly. "It's not an uncommon situation, Mr. Donaldson."

"Jay!"

"For tonight, then—Jay."

They were on the outskirts of the town now and he concentrated on his driving.

Mrs. Exe, still dressed as Mary Queen of Scots, entered the panelled bedroom from the lift, taking the timing clock from under her cloak. "Is he comfortable, dear?" she asked Hogan, who was helping himself to another whisky.

"No bother at all, Mother."

"Good." She went over to stare at the little man lying snoring on top of the coverlet. "Not much meat on his bones," she said disparagingly.

"No. Little and noisy."

She chuckled. "We'll soon put a stop to that." She wound the timer, moving the indicator to "Well done," and sat down by the fire as Hogan went to give the signal to Willie. When he had made sure that the bed-top was descending smoothly, Hogan went to sit beside his Mother. From a pocket in her capacious dress she produced a piece of crochet work.

"I wanted to have a word with you about Mr. White," she said, concentrating on her work.

"What's the trouble?"

"Nothing, really, but he's being a bit tiresome about reading matter."

"I'll have a word with him." He glanced round at the bed. The unconscious man was hidden from sight now.

"I wish you would. He doesn't seem to understand that we can't supply him all the time with fresh books. I mean, they're expensive."

"He's a great reader, but he doesn't read the right things. It's all frivolous stuff. A man should endeavour to improve his mind."

She leaned forward and patted his knee affectionately. "Yes, but not everyone's like you, dear." Her eyes were tender in their regard for her son. "They're not all as good as my Hoagy."

The dance had only just begun when Jay and Selina entered the decorated hall. He waited for her to come back from the cloakroom and felt a fresh thrill of admiration as she came towards him, looking rather shy. "I'll bet a hundred dollars you're the belle of the ball," he said enthusiastically.

After the first six dances he was still as sure that she was the loveliest girl in the room. Flushed, her eyes sparkling, she was enjoying every second of the occasion with an ever-increasing verve that made him study her uncertainly during the pause that was taking place after the last number. She seemed perhaps a little *too* animated; there was almost a touch of hysteria in her voice.

Maybe it was just that she wasn't used to champagne? They hadn't taken another drink for they had been dancing continuously, not even taking time off to sit at a table.

"Oh, Jay, this is marvellous, marvellous, *marvellous!*"

The band struck up again and she darted forward, dragging at his arm. "Come *on*; don't waste time! "

Smiling indulgently, he followed the eager girl and took her in his arms. He wasn't the best dancer in the world, but the floor was getting more crowded now and his mistakes weren't so obvious. Not that it mattered a great deal: Selina seemed able to follow his moves, even when they were highly original. They danced without speaking and when the last number was finished the M.C. announced an interval.

"Would you like a drink, or would you prefer a breath of fresh air?"

"Let's go outside. I couldn't *bear* to stand still or sit down."

"I'm glad you're enjoying it."

"Enjoying it! It's heaven!" She thrust an arm through his, hugging herself against it. In any other woman it would have been an open invitation, but with Selina he recognized a childlike innocent gesture of gratitude. "This is the first *real* dance I've been to for, oh, for years."

"You like dancing?"

She considered the question. "Not much, really, but it's just——" She stopped abruptly, some of the gaiety fading from her face.

"It's just—what?"

"Oh, nothing." She looked at him gravely. "Maybe it's all the people, the lights and music." They were at the end of the balcony now, with star-sprinkled darkness spread out before them.

"Why don't you get a job in a light, cheerful place, where you would meet a lot of people?"

"I have to stick to this job."

"It isn't the only one."

"It is for me." There was a trace of hardness in her voice. "At least, it is for the next three years. You see, Mr. Donaldson"—he let her use of his surname go without comment—"it'll take me at least another three years to get out of debt."

This time he was really shocked. "Debt?"

"Oh, nothing dishonourable, I assure you." She'd sensed

his reaction and he was annoyed with himself. He must have sounded like an outraged Puritan.

"I'm sorry."

"I'm the one who should be apologizing," she said flatly. It was hateful to spoil the evening in this way, but she couldn't help it. She wanted the American to know all about her now; if he was just amusing himself, he'd soon be scared off. "It's a very ordinary situation. After my Father died I found out he was in debt to Uncle Hogan. So I'm paying off the debt as best I can."

He hesitated. "Couldn't you get a better job somewhere else and pay the money off more quickly?"

"Perhaps."

"Then why in heaven's name don't you?"

"When I'm at Aarolie, Jay, I can get back home now and again." Her smile was gentle. "It's very lovely." Behind them, in the ballroom, the band struck up again, and her reaction was immediate.

"May I have a drink, please, and then I'd like to dance."

He followed her into the brightly-lit room, still puzzled over the almost feverish gaiety she was displaying, then he put aside his nagging doubts as he steered her towards the bar.

Willie launched the plastic-wrapped wire cage and its occupant on the journey along the ramp, saluting rigidly at attention until the bier disappeared from view. Then, as his father moved off to get the rowing-boat, Willie pulled out a tattered book from his pocket and handed it to Mrs. Exe.

"Here you are, Gran."

"Thank you, my dear." She smiled fondly at him. "You're a good boy, Willie."

The gown of Mary Queen of Scots was a little long and she had to hold her skirts up as she went through the labyrinth of passages and underground rooms, followed by Willie. She turned and frowned at him. "Aren't you forgetting something?"

He looked at her, his round face contorted with the effort of trying to remember. He gave up. "What is it, Gran?"

"You've got to go and get the special room ready for Mr. Donaldson."

"Oh, that! . . . I'd like to get it *really* ready for him."

"Now, Willie, that's not a nice thing to say. It's likely Mr. Donaldson will be with us for a long time yet. Years, maybe." She made a shooing motion. "Be off with you!" He did as she ordered and she continued her journey to the place where Charles White was kept.

"Good evening, Mr. White. Looks as though the rain's cleared, doesn't it?"

"Have you brought me something to read?" He was in a nervy, irritable mood that bordered on panic, for he knew only too well what she had been doing.

"We've just been seeing one of our guests off," she said placidly. "Not a very nice man. If he came again I wouldn't have him in the place."

"Have you brought me a book?"

"As a matter of fact, I've brought you two." From the depths of a pocket she produced a couple of tattered paperbacks, passing them over to where he could reach them. His eagerness made his hand tremble as he stretched out to fumble them towards him. He just managed it; an inch farther and he couldn't have touched the books, but she knew to a nicety where to place things for him to grasp. But the moment he saw what they were he gave a wail of frustration and anger.

"I've read them!"

"Have you? But I'm sure you'll enjoy them again as much."

White was shaking with fury. He threw one book on the table. "I've read that fifteen times," he shouted. Then he threw down the second one. "And I've read that seventeen times!"

"Have you now! " She regarded him with concern. "You mustn't read so much, Mr. White. You'll get eyestrain." She looked down at the lurid covers of the two paperbacks. One depicted a terrified girl in bridal dress being menaced by bats that had human faces, and was entitled *Terror in the Night*. The other was called *Prisoners of the Creatures*, and showed a terrified girl tied to a stake and being menaced by three-eyed giants in human form.

White was weeping helplessly now. "Come, come, no tears," she admonished him. "Life's too short for misery." She took the book Willie had given her and placed it on the table. "Here, maybe this will cheer you up."

It was a little time before he looked up and then he saw the book. It was a struggle to reach it, but he managed it at last and stared at it as though unable to believe his good fortune. "Thank you, oh, thank you," he stammered.

"Make it last, now," she warned. "We can't expect treats every day, can we?" Nodding happily to herself, she withdrew, but White wasn't even aware of her going. He was gazing in an ecstasy of anticipation at the cover of the book, which bore, in old-fashioned type, the words:

The Traveller's Story of a Terribly Strange Bed
and Other Stories
by Wilkie Collins

Reverently he turned to the first page and began to read.

Hogan tied up the boat at the landing stage and went into the castle. Willie was waiting for him. "Everything all right, son?"

"Yes, Dad."

"The Yankee back yet?"

"No."

"Where's your Gran?"

"In the bar."

"Then let's go and have a drink, eh? I reckon we've earned one." Hogan led the way self-importantly to the bar. Tonight's business had been a sign that things were starting to come right for him. The little man, Creighton, had been a gift from the skies.

The bar was in darkness except for a solitary light over the tiny counter. Mrs. Exe was intent on polishing glasses, head bent to one side to avoid the smoke from the cigarette that dangled from her bottom lip; a glass with a generous measure of rum in it near at hand. "All clear, Hoagy?"

"All clear."

"Splendid. Then you'll be needing a drink."

"Can I have one, Gran?"

She regarded Willie solemnly, head still tilted on one side. "If your Father says so." Hogan nodded and she turned back to her grandson. "What'll it be?"

He gave the matter some thought, then decided. "Port and tomato juice."

"Very well, dear."

"And can I have a cherry in it?"

"I think we might manage that, lad."

She emptied her own glass, downing the three fingers of rum without blinking, then set about pouring drinks for all of them.

The glasses charged, she passed them out, raising her own in a toast.

"To the Club! "

They drank ceremoniously, then Hogan put his empty glass down. "Time for bed, Willie. You'll have to be up before dawn and get rid of that car."

Chapter Fourteen

THE evening had been wonderful. Selina was laughing almost continuously, full of high spirits, and then she saw the clock above the platform. "Two o'clock!" she gasped. "That's never right!"

He steered her round a couple who were indulging in the execution of complicated and uncertain steps. "It's a couple of minutes fast."

The laughter died from her face. "I must go back."

"There's another hour yet."

"Not for me." She stood still and now everyone had to steer round them. "It'll be three before we get back to Aarolie, and I have to be up at six."

"I thought you were enjoying yourself?"

"I've had a wonderful evening, but please, I want to go home now." She looked distressed. "I never dreamed it was so late."

He accepted her decision with as much grace as he could muster, although it was very difficult to adjust to her mercurial changes of mood. She was serious now, more like the remote and depressed girl he'd first met at the castle. But perhaps he was being unfair. It was easy enough for him if, in the morning, he felt tired. Selina, though, would have to put in a full day's work—probably more, in order to catch up. The hotel wasn't exactly overstaffed.

The drive back to the castle was silent and, from Jay's point of view, an anticlimax. Selina sat huddled, with her coat collar turned up and without speaking and with every mile he drove she seemed to become more and more withdrawn and remote. He had the impression that if he asked a question she would call him "sir" when she answered.

It was a relief when he saw, ahead of him, a light being waved from side to side. Someone was flagging him down and as he slowed he could see in the headlights that the signaller was Tam Bruce.

"Hello there, Mr. Bruce! "

"Och, it'll be Mr. Donaldson."

"Anything wrong?"

"No, sir, just that I wanted to check who was abroad." Bruce peered into the car. "Ye'll be coming back from the ball?"

"I thought we might see you there, Mr. Bruce."

The policeman took the suggestion seriously. "I'd ma duty to do, sir. 'Twould be a grand night for the poachers to be oot and aboot."

Jay kept his expression solemn. "We haven't seen any, I'm afraid."

"Aye, well." He drew back. "Good night to ye both."

"Good night."

As he started the car up again, Jay laughed. "You have to give him credit! Poachers! "

"He could be right."

He spared a quick glance at her, surprised. "You think so?" But her moment of animation had passed and she was silent again until they reached the castle. The blazing headlights lit up the great grey façade of the building. "You'd get a marvellous effect if the place was flood-lit," he said.

Selina was out of the car almost before he'd brought it to a halt. Her face showed no expression at all as she looked directly at him for a moment. "Thank you very much. It was a wonderful evening. Wonderful. . . . Good night, sir."

He stared after her in hurt indignation as she hurried off. "Hey! What the hell . . . ! " But she had gone from sight, into the building. Frowning in annoyance he steered the Bentley round to the lean-to garage. The spot he had occupied earlier was taken up by another car, one he hadn't seen before. Apparently there was a new guest at the hotel.

Jay parked the silver-grey convertible then walked slowly back to the entrance. It was a perfect night, with an almost full moon; the sky clear and star-studded, and he'd been a dolt not to take advantage of the opportunity. A short row on the loch would have been perfect. But now . . . bed was the only thing left.

The entrance-hall was dimly lit and felt eerie as he crossed it to mount the grand staircase. When he got to his room he was surprised to see the fire was still alight, and even more surprised when he came to take the various things from his pockets and lay them on the dressing-table. None of the objects already on the top of the dressing-table was in the place where he had left it. Everything had been moved.

In the bathroom, too, things had been shifted from where he had put them. He might have believed he was imagining it all, until he opened the drawer where he had placed his clean socks and found it full of shirts. In all his life he had used a *left*-hand drawer for socks. Now they were in the right-hand one. He rubbed his chin, reflecting.

"Willie?"

Selina climbed into bed, lay down and stared blindly up at the ceiling. Slowly, tears began to well from her eyes and run down over her temples. "I'm sorry, Jay," she whispered. She knew he must be offended by the way she'd behaved and she would have given a great deal to try and mend the damage. But nothing was simple for her and there was much that was frightening. And he was so kind. . . . The tears came faster with the memory of his kindness. "I'm sorry . . . sorry."

She switched out the bedside lamp, then rolled over on to her face so that her sobs were muffled as she thumped the pillow in despair with the small, clenched fist. "Damn,

damn, damn! "

When the first streaks of dawn lit the sky she was awake, miserably going over all the things she had done wrong on her evening out. She'd behaved like a—like a gauche school-girl. If the American even looked at her again, she'd be lucky. Suddenly she heard the muffled noise of a car engine and she sat up, already convinced that Jay, never wanting to speak to her again, was leaving.

"Jay! "

She swung her legs out of bed and ran across to the window. By leaning right out she could see the fore-court with the inn sign. Sixty feet below her there was a car she hadn't seen before. It had a red bonnet and a white roof and as she watched, Willie came into view. He was wheeling a bicycle and, opening the boot of the car, he put the machine in.

Then he went and climbed into the driver's seat and started the engine. She knew she'd been silly to imagine it was the Bentley. This car had a noisy engine, as though it was on the verge of breaking down, whereas you couldn't hear the Bentley's engine at all. She was just withdrawing her head when Willie started off in the red-and-white car.

For a long time she crouched beside the open window, staring at the spot where the car had disappeared round a bend in the narrow drive. Whose car was it Willie was driving? And why was he taking it away at such an early hour? Shivering, she went back to bed and almost immediately fell asleep.

Willie drove the red-and-white vehicle down to the cattle grid, where he stopped and got out to make sure that the main road was deserted. Satisfied, he got back into the driver's seat and turned left, on to the road. The road passed through a plantation of pines, planted fifteen years earlier, and a mile farther on he turned left on to a track that had been cleared of trees to form a fire-break.

The track rose steeply and became narrower. Where there

were wire baskets containing twig brooms to be used as fire-beaters, it was difficult to get the car past.

Its engine was making a harsh clanking noise and now he was worried in case it should fail completely. But luck was with him. The trees were thinner now, with occasional rocks jutting from the soil, and then he was at the spot where he had to stop.

Ahead of him the track ran between two humps of rock, then opened out into a smooth expanse of green; the flat surface of which was walled in by surrounding outcrops of sheer granite. He went to the boot and took the bicycle out, propping it carefully against one of the humps of rock, then got back in the vehicle, revving the noisy engine and putting it in gear.

The car shot forward, between the walls of granite and out on to the smooth green. It had travelled no more than four or five yards when it came to a halt, the wheels sinking into the greenness of the bog, as the car began to settle. Laughing wildly, Willie scrambled out of the open door and up on to the car roof, where he stood for a moment, steadying himself with outstretched arms.

Carefully, he shuffled to the back of the roof and squatting to let himself down on to the boot he took a flying leap from it on to firm ground. He went sprawling and for a moment lay there, laughing convulsively, before scrambling to his feet.

Already the car was half immersed in the green slime; within two or three more minutes it would be out of sight. He picked up a few pieces of rock and amused himself by throwing them at the car, smashing the rear window. But then the excitement was over; with one last gurgle the car roof disappeared below the surface and the deadly bog looked as it had done before he sent the car plunging on to the treacherous stuff. Willie stiffened to attention and saluted. "Sunk without trace, Admiral," he stated solemnly. "And no survivors."

He went over to the nearest wire basket and took one of the fire-fighting brooms from it, using the twiggy implement to brush out the car's tyre tracks. When he was satisfied that the tracks were no longer visible, he replaced the broom and mounted the bicycle making a wobbly start on the journey back home.

When Selina woke she turned over luxuriously to go to sleep again when she saw through half-closed eyes the hands of the little travelling clock she kept beside her bed. They registered the time as being six forty-eight. Unbelievingly she stared at it; fully awake now as she realized that either the alarm had failed, or she had slept through it.

"Oh, lord!"

Groaning, she forced herself to get out of bed and began to stagger round, trying to make up for lost time. When she had washed and dressed she looked at the costume she had worn at the dance, staring at it musingly for a moment, then, shrugging, she picked it up and went along to Mrs. Exe's room to return it. There was no reply when she knocked on the door and after a moment's hesitation she went in.

Mrs. Exe was not there; she was probably in the kitchen already. The room was in its usual muddle, with a length of material that the old woman was making into something, in a heap on the floor beside the sewing-machine. Selina picked up the material to drape it over a chair and was surprised to see two suitcases which appeared to have been hidden under the cloth. They were light-coloured and bore the initials G.C. embossed in gold letters.

The only other free space in the room was on the bed and she placed the costume on it lingeringly before leaving to go down to the day's tasks. She was wondering how Jay would greet her, what he would say and what his manner would be. Should she apologize for leaving him so abruptly, or would it be better not to mention it at all?

But she didn't get the opportunity to find out, for he

163

didn't come in for breakfast. An awful, nagging suspicion that he had left the hotel made her take the time off to find out if the Bentley was still in the lean-to. It was, and she felt a tremendous surge of relief as she saw it.

"Looking for something?"

It was Willie, working on some piece of machinery or electrical equipment at the back of the garage. "No." She wasn't in the mood to talk to the youth and she went back inside. He watched her until she was out of sight, then mimicked her in an exaggerated walk, breaking off to put out his tongue after her.

Willie returned to his task and was soldering two pieces of wire on to a switch when he heard someone else enter the lean-to. This time it was the American, come to check the oil and battery levels in his car.

"Hello, Captain."

Jay looked up briefly. "Morning, Willie." It was a mistake; he should have ignored the youth, for now Willie came shambling over, grinning with pleasure, to push his head under the open bonnet.

"Lovely piece of engineering, Admiral." There was genuine admiration in his voice; he was peering at it with the devotion of a mother regarding her first-born. Somehow the youth's attitude seemed pathetic to the man.

"You like engines?"

"I'm building one."

"Are you now! " Jay was tolerant in his attitude. "What sort of engine?"

Willie stood up and looked round as though making sure he could not be overheard. "I'm making a space ship," he whispered.

"A—a space ship?" For the first time Jay stared at him keenly. It had never occurred to him before that the young man was anything more than a bit light in the brain-box, but now . . . ? Was Willie serious, or was this another of his jokes?

164

"What fuel are you going to use?" He asked the question straight-faced.

"I've not got round to that yet." Willie was intense; the man of science. "I'm working on the launching problem."

"That must be quite something."

"I've thought of something no one else has." Willie moved closer, and spoke confidentially: "I'm going to launch my ship from the bottom of the sea. I'm going to put it down there, deep as I can go. Then I fill it with air and it'll shoot up to the surface, gathering speed all the time. It'll leap right out of the water, do you see, and at the moment it does, I'll cut in the rockets."

"Very interesting." Jay closed the bonnet and then became aware that Willie was staring at him triumphantly.

"You don't understand, do you?"

"Understand what?"

"When my space ship leaves the water it'll be travelling at a thousand miles an hour accelerating all the way and all done by the water, I reckon, so there'll be no inertia to overcome; just a matter of increasing the acceleration. That way you can cut down on rocket fuel and increase the pay load, or you can have the conventional amount of fuel and build up your speed so you can break away from the earth's gravitational field." He smiled proudly. "I shall go to Venus and prove the Yanks were wrong when they said no one lives on Venus."

Jay had heard enough. He patted the youth on the shoulder and got into the driving-seat. "You're a bright boy, Willie. Very bright." He started the engine.

Willie stared after the disappearing car, the good-humour leaving his expression. "You ain't smart enough to understand, are you! No, the only thing you can do is to threaten to beat people up."

Hogan Exe was in a tremendously good mood. He was waiting in the kitchen, tasting the contents of the various saucepans by dipping a finger in them and sucking it clean, when Mrs. Exe returned from a trip to the wine-cellars. She had a dozen full bottles of claret in a basket which she dumped on the table.

"We're going to need some more white wine, Hoagy."

"I'll order some to-day. I'm going into town."

She stared at him, surprised. "Going into town?"

He smirked at her. "Just to celebrate."

"That's nice. What is there to celebrate, or is it a secret?"

He put his arm round her shoulders, fondly. "I've just pulled off a nice piece of business. . . . The Yank's just agreed to buy a stretch of the river."

She was delighted. "That's marvellous."

"He's just this minute gone off to make arrangements for the money."

"How much?"

"Ten thousand dollars."

"How much is that in real money?"

"Over three thousand pounds."

She shook her head doubtfully. "It's not much, is it? I mean, he's worth a million."

"It's as much as we can get our hands on."

"Well, I don't think it's worth it, dear. There's bound to be an awful fuss made when he disappears. I mean, he's really someone, isn't he?"

Hogan flushed, all his pleasure evaporating in a moment. "You're never satisfied!"

"Look, dear, I'm only telling you for your own good——"

"It's three thousand pounds, Ma. How the hell could we get our hands on that much money in any other way? They won't let you. Not those damned capitalists. You know that. Look at the way they treated me!" He was working himself into a rage and she tried to soothe him.

"All right, dear, your old Mother was wrong."

But he broke loose from the hand she placed on his arm.

"You're always trying to spoil everything." He glared at her for a moment then wheeled and hurried out of the kitchen. For a moment she stared after him, then started to shake her head in disapproval.

Hogan rushed out from the kitchen, nearly knocking Selina over. He didn't stop to apologize; he didn't even seem to notice that he had bumped into her and a moment later she heard the roar of the shooting-brake's engine. She moved to the door just in time to see him racing off down the drive.

Hogan's burst of ill-temper passed as suddenly as it had appeared. By the time he reached the road he was chuckling. He felt in his coat pocket and brought out the wad of ten-pound notes that he had taken from Creighton's suitcase, putting the money down on the seat beside him, where he could touch it and see it while he drove. Already he was licking his dry lips in anticipation of the drinks he was going to take in order to celebrate the latest kill.

"Latest kill! " he shouted aloud. The words amused him, and he laughed savagely.

After he dismounted from his heavy and ancient bicycle, Tam Bruce was disconcerted to learn that Hogan Exe was not at the castle. It looked as if he was going to miss his medicinal tot, although today, with the sky clear blue and only a gentle breeze tempering the heat, it would have been difficult to find an excuse for taking the medicine.

Tam was at his most official, grave and concerned with the task in hand as he sent Willie to fetch his Grandmother. Mrs. Exe came into the entrance-hall, wiping floury hands on a cloth.

"Yes, Tam, what is it?"

"I'm here on official business, Mrs. Exe." The gravity of his tone failed to impress her.

"We haven't seen any poachers, Tam."

"Ah'm no' here aboot poachers, Mrs. Exe." From his

breast pocket he took out a notebook and opened it, then stared down at her. "It's aboot a missing person." He cleared his throat, and began to read aloud: "Gordon Creighton, aged forty-four. Five foot four inches tall. Eight stones in weight." He looked up from his notebook. "Did anyone of that description call here last night?"

She was blandly innocent. "Good heavens, no! . . . Should he have done?"

"The mannie's missing. All the police have been told to look out for him. . . . You havena' seen him?"

"No. . . . What's he done?"

"Done?"

"Is he running away from the police?"

"No, Mam, he isn't. It's thought he might have met with —with an accident."

"Could he have lost his memory?"

"It's possible."

Willie was peering round the edge of the doorway, watching the constable, and Mrs. Exe summoned him. "There's a man missing, Willie."

"What's he done, Gran? Is Mr. Bruce going to arrest him?"

The policeman hastened to put the youth right. "No, lad, nothing like that. He'd a lot of valuables on him, and he's a-missing."

Willie appeared to be awed. "Someone's robbed and murdered him, I'll bet."

Mrs. Exe was quick to agree. "That's very likely, Willie." She turned to the constable. "You're not safe anywhere these days."

"Murder!" Bruce was aghast. There was no murder in their part of the world—leastways, not of human beings. There were plenty of deer and fish killed, and many of those illegally, but as for human beings . . . !" He returned the notebook to his pocket and prepared to leave; there were duties to be performed.

"Well, if he does turn up, maybe you'd be good enough to inform me." He caught a suspicion of movement in the corner of his vision and turned to see the girl, Selina. He smiled at her. "You got home safely, then, lass?"

She paused. "Yes, thank you." She moved on, frowning, and straining to hear his next words to Mrs. Exe and Willie.

"Gordon Creighton, that's his name. And he's driving a red-and-white car."

"Red and white——" Selina whispered, her frown deepening. She had passed through the doorway now, but stopped and turned back to listen. But the policeman was moving towards the entrance, his back to her, and she couldn't hear what he was saying for his deep voice was no more than a mumble.

When Jay returned to the castle the place seemed deserted. He'd missed tea, but the fact didn't bother him, and he went straight up to his room. There, stuck on the mirror of the dressing-table by a bit of stamp paper, was a note. He didn't recognize the writing, but it must be Selina's. The note was brief:

Please, I must talk with you as soon as possible. "S."

He frowned over the message for a moment, trying to speculate on its meaning, then put it in his pocket and went up to the floor above, to her bedroom. But there was no answer to his knocking and after a few moments' wait, he went back to his own room.

It wasn't until he went down to the dining-room that he saw her. She was busy preparing the tables for dinner, laying out the cutlery. He pushed open the door and went across to where she was intent on her job.

"You wanted to see me?"

She gave a nervous start, dropping a bundle of knives from her hand. Something was wrong; she looked tired, but that was natural enough, after the late night. But there was something else. She looked . . . frightened.

"Not now," she said feverishly, looking towards the door.

"What's wrong?"

"I—I can't tell you here." She looked ghastly and was trembling. "Can you come to my room, in fifteen minutes?"

"If that'll help."

"Yes. Fifteen minutes. Now go," she begged him.

Jay left the dining-room and went outside to give thought to the matter. Willie swooped past, riding an imaginary motor-cycle, accelerating into the entrance-hall without even noticing the American. The youth was not quite sane; Jay realized that now. And what about Selina? Were her rapid changes of mood due to some mental unbalance?

But he shuddered away from the thought.

Chapter Fifteen

SELINA opened the door of her bedroom and almost dragged Jay inside. "I can't spare more than five minutes," she said urgently, "but I *must* talk to someone."

"Go ahead."

"I—I think there are some sort of crooks working here."

"Crooks? You mean cardsharps?" He thought of the invitations to join the evening poker games he'd always refused.

"Poachers."

It was so much of an anticlimax that he laughed. "Is that all?"

But Selina seemed merely irritated by his light-hearted attiude. "Listen. Mr. Bruce was up here today, just after lunch. The police are looking for a man named Creighton —Gordon Creighton. My Aunt said she'd never heard of him. *But he stayed here, at Aarolie, last night!*"

"How do you know?"

"There's some suitcases in Aunty's room, with the initials 'G.C.' on them."

It was difficult for Jay not to be scornful. "That's a bit thin, isn't it? There must be thousands of 'G.C.'s."

"It's the same man, I know it is." She was getting a little stubborn, he could tell by the set of her jaw and by the way her eyes glittered. "I saw his car—red and white, it was."

"Red and white?" He pulled at his lower lip thoughtfully. There'd been a two-tone job in the lean-to when he'd parked the Bentley in the small hours. "What does that prove?"

"I don't know. That's what I want you to tell me." She went on defiantly. "I saw Willie drive off in that car, about five o'clock this morning, or earlier. He took a bicycle with him and he wasn't away long, because he was here for breakfast."

If he had been told the story twenty-four hours earlier he would have dismissed it as none of his business. But there were several factors that needed explanation. While he and Selina were away for the evening, for instance, someone had moved everything in his room.

"What do you reckon?"

"I don't know, but I'm scared. I mean, why lie to the police? If Uncle had done that, or even Willie, I wouldn't have thought anything. But Aunty!"

He studied her for a moment, wondering. "Have you told me everything?"

"No," she admitted reluctantly. "I think Uncle's keeping someone hidden, somewhere in the castle. Aunty's always carrying off trays of food and I'm sure she doesn't eat the stuff herself. . . . I think there's a gang of poachers and they're using Aarolie as a headquarters. Mr. Bruce suspects something, he's always up here. But I don't suppose he's able to prove anything."

"Have you spoken to him about this?"

"How could I? I don't want to get Aunty into trouble with the police."

It was too big a problem to be solved immediately. The first thing he had to do was to consider whether Selina's story was true. There was little or nothing to support it, but his own experience with the Exes made him think carefully before putting it all down to the imagination of a slightly hysterical girl.

There was what had happened to the things in his room —and the business of Hogan Exe's under-the-counter deal. That very afternoon Jay had made arrangements for the equivalent of an extra ten thousand dollars to be made available for him in cash. If the Exes *were* crooked . . . ? For the time being he decided to make no mention of the money; Selina would, no doubt, judge him to be a sucker.

If it had been anyone else he would have dropped the whole thing, probably packed his grips there and then and left. But he was too involved now; they were in something together—whatever it was. She was peering anxiously at the little clock beside her bed.

"I—I shall have to go in a minute." She looked him levelly in the eyes. "You think I'm making a fuss over nothing, don't you?"

It was a bit too close to the truth to be comfortable. "It isn't that, Selina. We've no proof."

"All right, if that's what you want, I'll see if I can find some . . . . Wait here."

There was a new determination in her voice and her movements were decisive as she opened the door and disappeared along the corridor. He didn't have long to wait. She was back within seconds, waving something triumphantly before his face.

"Well, what about this?"

He took the object from her. It was a leather wallet, old and stained with use and, from the feel of it, almost empty. But there were one or two papers inside—a driver's licence, a motor-car certificate of insurance, and a tennis club membership card.

All three of them were made out in the name of Gordon Creighton.

"Gordon Creighton! " he said slowly, then looked up at her. "So you were right."

But she wasn't interested in victory. "What do we do?"

He handed her the wallet. "Put this back for the time being. I'll think it over and we'll decide after dinner."

"Dinner! Good lord! I must fly." She grabbed the wallet and went pelting out of the room along to Mrs. Exe's. It took only a second to replace the wallet; it had taken her no longer to find it, for it had lain on top of the clothes in the first case she'd opened.

She went speeding past Jay who was standing in the doorway of her room, and down the spiral stairs, followed more slowly by the American, his head bent in grave thought.

As Jay reached the next floor he was watched by Willie, who was peering out of his slightly opened door. When Jay had gone out of sight, Willie went back to his room and switched off the loudspeaker through which he had heard every word of the conversation between the American and the girl.

"Report to Headquarters, Commander," he told himself aloud. "Report to Headquarters."

He went in search of his Gran, to tell her all that he had overheard.

Jay waited impatiently in the public phone booth in the entrance-hall, waiting to be put through to the number he had asked for. At last he heard the deep, Scottish tones of the policeman's voice.

"Hello, Mr. Bruce, this is——"

"Mr. Donaldson."

"That's right." Jay was impressed by the other's quick certainty.

"What can I do for you, sir?"

"Oh, it's nothing much. . . . One of the folks here told me you're looking for a missing guy. Name of Clayton."

"Not Clayton, sir. Creighton. Gordon Creighton."

"Creighton, eh?" He managed a laugh. "Then it can't be the guy I mean. I met someone named Clayton the other day, and I was wondering. . . ."

"Not the same mannie, sir."

Blast the constable! Didn't he ever volunteer information? "Er—was there any reason you want him? Apart from the fact that he's missing, I mean."

"There's also the matter of valuable property, sir. That's missing also." He paused. "But I told this to Mrs. Exe, ye ken. She'll tell you all about it, if you want to know, sir."

Jay hung up, not at all certain what he should do. He went in search of Selina, but couldn't find her. Seeing Willie come from the direction of the kitchen, he called to him. "Have you any idea where Selina is?"

Willie grinned, looking over Donaldson's shoulder to where Mrs. Exe was peeping round the door jamb, watching. "She's gone down to the wine-cellar, Admiral."

"Go and tell her I'd like a word with her as soon as possible."

"Aye, aye, sir."

He hurried off, back to his grandmother, who caught his arm and held him there, giving herself time to think. "I wish your Father was here. He'd know what to do."

"The Yank's just made a phone call, Gran. Suppose it was to the police?"

"Yes. If Bruce comes snooping, we must make sure he doesn't find out any more." Her mind was made up. "All right, you know what to do, Willie, dear."

"Can't we fix her after dinner, Gran?" he pleaded. "Then she can see to the serving. . . . I'm fed up with doing her work."

She regarded him sternly. "Be a good boy and do as you're told. Go on. Shoo! "

Donaldson had gone. Up to his room? She hurried across to the great staircase, mounting as quickly as possible and, panting with the exertion, made for his room. If there was going to be any trouble with the American she wanted to make him as helpless as possible. If she had spared another look down into the great hall he would have seen Jay re-enter and glance up to see her.

But Mrs. Exe was intent on her errand. Reaching the American's room, she tapped on the door, listening for any reply. Jay turned the corner of the corridor just in time to see her stoop to peer through the keyhole, then knock again. He drew back to observe her, wondering just what she was up to.

A moment later she opened the door and entered the room. He waited where he was, trying to decide whether to go and catch her at whatever she was doing, or to confront her when she came out.

Mrs. Exe's visit to the room didn't need more than a few seconds. Donaldson had a leather, hand-tooled case containing a pair of shotguns and another case containing a sporting rifle, fitted with telescopic sights. She picked up the two cases and went to the secret lift. When she got to the dungeons she rushed away, pushing the lift gate to, but failing to close it in her hurry. There was a great deal to be seen to.

Jay's patience soon ran out. He moved down the corridor and let himself into the bedroom, throwing open the door with a sudden movement designed to disconcert the old lady. But he was the one to be disconcerted: the room was empty. "Where the hell . . . !"

But not until he had looked in the bathroom and in the wardrobe—and even tried to peer under the four-poster— did he admit to himself that Mrs. Exe had vanished. He gazed round, wondering what had caused her to visit the room, but failed to notice that the weapons were missing.

Slowly and thoughtfully, shaking his head in defeat, he left the bedroom and went down to the huge entrance-hall. The moment he set foot on the stone floor, Willie came rushing out. 'Selina's had an accident!'" His face was glistening with a sweat of fear and for a moment Jay felt a surge of rage.

"If you've been up to your tricks . . . !"

"She fell down. In the wine-cellar."

"Show me the way." The youth was motionless, staring.

"Show me the way!" Jay yelled. He could have murdered the dolt.

Willie went off at a shambling run, leading the American. It was perfectly done and he had no suspicion that he was moving into a trap. Willie was beckoning him. "This way, Admiral." They went down the stairs to the entrance to the cellars, and Willie moved ahead at a shuffling trot between the rows of bins to where Selina was lying, unconscious.

Jay went down on his knee beside her, looking for signs of injury, but there was none visible. Willie spoke. "The floor's not very warm in here. Can we take her through there?" It was the first sensible suggestion Jay had ever heard from the youth and he was grateful. Tenderly he gathered the limp girl into his arms and stood up with her, following Willie again.

The youth passed through an arch, the door that fitted it was four-inch-thick oak studded with iron pegs. As the dim overhead light went on, Jay glanced round the bare cellar, then looked at Willie, who was standing expectantly in the middle of the stone floor, with an expression on his face that Jay couldn't interpret. Then the man heard the door behind him slam shut, the bolts creaking into place.

"What the hell!"

Willie started to chuckle. "Gran's shut us out of the . . ."

Dreadful suspicion gripped Jay. "How do we get out of here?" There were three others doors in the place, all shut, and he glanced at each of them in turn. He was going to speak again, but felt the girl stir in his arms. Then she opened her eyes and moaned slightly. He put her down, steadying her with one arm as she looked round her, still dazed.

"Are you all right?"

"Wh—what happened?" She winced, feeling her jaw with gentle fingers. Then her eyes widened. "Willie! He hit me!"

Jay suffered a moment of hatred for the youth. He could

177

kill . . . But when he looked round, Willie had gone. Then, echoing through the dungeon came the sound of his mad, booming laughter.

Chapter Sixteen

HOGAN EXE had enjoyed his day out. He was in a mellow temper as he drove back towards Aarolie and when he came in sight of Bruce's cottage he decided to stop, as he often did, to pass the time of day and have another tot with the policeman. Bruce, in shirt-sleeves and reading a newspaper, got up to welcome his caller, his greeting slightly the warmer for the sight of the whisky bottle Hogan was carrying up the garden path.

"Anybody at home?"

"Come away in, Mr. Exe."

Exe entered, tripping slightly over the doorstep; he had been celebrating his stroke of good fortune all day and had drunk enough whisky to paralyse three lesser men. "I thought we'd have a wee dram, Tam." He sniggered. "Poetry! "

Bruce eyed his caller. He'd never seen the big man in such a cheerful mood. Not that Tam approved of cheerfulness. Life was a serious business. Drinking whisky was also a serious business. He put two mugs on the bare table with due solemnity and watched, gravely approving, as the bearded man poured out generous measures.

"Slanch! "

"Good health! "

The drink went down smoothly and rapidly, then Exe was refilling the mugs. "Ye'll have been out to the town, Mr. Exe?"

"Yes. Business."

"Aye, aye. . . . Business is good?"

"Can't grumble."

"Aye, aye. . . . I called at Aarolie, the day."

Hogan laughed. "Still after your poachers?"

"It was another matter, Mr. Exe. A mannie, a forei—an Englishman, has gone a-missing." He sipped his whisky. "But your guid Mother told me he hadna' been to the castle."

"A missing man?" Hogan's hand was steady as he put the question. The sudden shrilling of the telephone bell made him jump, despite the control he was exerting. Bruce went over to the wall-telephone and lifted the receiver. Mrs. Exe on the other end of the line sounded distraught.

"Mr. Bruce? Do you happen to have seen my son anywhere on the road? He's later than he said he'd be."

Bruce turned to Exe. "'Tis your Mother, asking."

Hogan took the receiver. "Yes, Mother, what is it?"

Mrs. Exe's voice came over the line softly. "Hoagy, dear, come home right away, will you?"

He had rather fancied a session with the policeman. "I'll be back in an hour or two."

"No, Hoagy, that won't do. By that time we'll be in real trouble. . . . You understand? . . . Real trouble."

It was clear enough that something was wrong. "All right, I'll come straight away." He put the receiver on the hook, turning to face the watching man. "Well, Tam, I'm afraid I'll have to go. Mother's having a bit of trouble over the dinner. You know how it is?"

He was about to pick up the half-empty bottle of whisky, then hesitated. Obviously there was something wrong at the castle in which case he didn't want the copper snooping round there. If he left the rest of the whisky, Bruce would get himself into a stupor.

"I'll leave this with you."

For a moment Bruce was silent. Then: "That's verra guid of you, Mr. Exe. I appreciate it." He followed the hotel owner out of the cottage and down to where the shooting-brake was parked. There were a great many things piled in the back; Exe must have spent an awful lot of money that day.

As the vehicle moved off, Tam was staring at one of the items in the back, a drum of heavy-gauge wire. The policeman didn't know it, but the previous night's stroke of good fortune had made Hogan rather more ambitious.

The situation should have induced in Jay more apprehension than in fact it did. Selina seemed to be almost fully recovered from the blow Willie had dealt her on the chin. "I was just checking the bottles of wine," she mumbled. "Just checking, that's all. Then up he came for no reason, and hit me!" She felt her jaw with exploratory fingers. "I'm going to have a fine old bruise there tomorrow."

"We'll bother about that later. For the moment we'd better concentrate on getting out of here." He looked at each door in turn. "Which one?"

"I don't know. I've never been in here before. Only the wine-cellars."

"O.K., then. We'll find out." Taking her by the hand, he led her to the door straight ahead of them. It opened creakingly as he turned the iron ring that served as a handle. Beyond it there was darkness.

Leaving her, he went into the farther chamber and fumbled for a light switch. There was none, but his searching fingers encountered a lantern and some matches. He had just grasped them when the light in the other dungeon went out and Selina gave a stifled scream.

"It's all right," he said swiftly. "Stay where you are and I'll have a light in a second." Actually it took a little longer than that. The first match broke, the second one fizzled out before he could examine the lamp. But in the light of the third one he was able to see the hurricane lamp that was hanging from a nail on the wall. Half a minute later he managed to light the lamp, just as the sound of Willie's distant laughter came echoing through the dungeon.

Selina was staring at him in the lamplight, her eyes wide with fear. "What do you think's going to happen?"

Jay had no intention of telling her the truth. "I don't *think,* I know. I'm going to beat the living daylights out of Willie the moment we're out of here."

"You—you think we'll get out?"

"Of course, don't be silly!" Even to his own ears the words sounded strained and false.

"But if they're *really* crooks . . . ?" Her face was tense with strain and she had difficulty in forcing herself to speak. "If—if Uncle Hogan . . ." She halted, gulping, "I've never told this to anyone before. . . . Two years ago there was a—a guest at the hotel. He—liked me. Asked me to go out with him. Then, after he left, he came back unexpectedly one night. Just to see me. Uncle nearly killed him. Pretended he thought John—pretended he thought the man was a burglar. The things he did to him were terrible. I—I never saw or heard from John again."

She was trembling now. "I saw what Uncle did. I—I think he must have been mad." The recollection of the brutal attack made her shudder. "So don't you see . . . if he catches us . . . !"

"Look, girl, this is just one of Willie's jokes. A bit more vicious than usual, but that's all." They had wasted more than enough time already. When Hogan arrived back, that would be the time to get really worried. But Hogan might already be here. Jay pushed the thought to the back of his mind. "Come on."

He grasped her wrist with one hand, holding the lantern high above his head with the other. Its dim light failed to penetrate the darkness for any distance, and there was nothing to give him guidance. Slowly he moved forward, straining to see into the gloom, pulling the reluctant girl with him. When he had gone some distance he saw something glint ahead of him. It was another lantern, hung on the wall beside a further doorway.

With the second lantern alight and being carried by Selina, things improved somewhat. "Stay here," he said, and continued along the wall. There was another door, then another—probably the one they had come through. He looked down at the stone floor and saw the line of footprints he and the girl had made in the dust.

By the time he completed the tour of the dungeons' walls he had come across a fourth doorway and when he reached her side again he tried to figure out which one to try. He had no idea in which direction he was headed, but if they kept straight on, perhaps they would come to an exit from the dungeons.

"We'll go this way," he decided. But once in the farther chamber, his idea had to be scrapped. The wall immediately ahead was blank, without a doorway. Instead, there were several sets of iron rings bolted into the granite, with chains dangling from them. The place they were in now was probably where men were chained and imprisoned hundreds of years ago.

Selina was pressing herself against him, shivering. She had seen the chains, but made no comment. "How about left?" he said buoyantly, trying to cheer her up a little. But again he was thwarted. The iron-studded oaken door was either locked or bolted. He threw himself against it and might, for all the effect it had, have been throwing himself against the solid granite of the walls and floor.

"No good that way."

Fortunately the door on the other side of the chamber was unfastened. He opened it and jumped back, swearing in fright as a human skeleton swung out at him. Selina gave a wild shriek, almost fainting, as the thing dangled in the doorway.

Hogan drove up to the castle at top speed, slammed his

foot on the brake pedal and brought the vehicle to a sliding halt. Almost before it had stopped he was out, running towards the entrance. He found his Mother in the kitchen, passing dishes of vegetables through to a sullen-faced Willie, in the dining-room.

"What's wrong?"

"The American knows about Creighton. Selina must have told him."

"How the hell did *she* know?" He made a gesture with one huge hand. "No, never mind that now. Have you fixed them?"

"They're both locked in the dungeons."

"Alive?"

"We didn't have time to deal with them, Hoagy. There was the dinner to be served."

He relaxed. "Well, if they're in the cellars, they won't get out. They can stay there until we can get at 'em."

"I'll make a special brew of coffee so the other guests won't hear anything if there's a noise." She smiled at him. "I'm glad you're back, boy." She took a pile of dirty soup plates from Willie. "I wasn't quite sure how to handle it. I got the American's guns."

He patted her approvingly on the shoulder. "I don't know what we should do without you, Ma, and that's a fact." Everything was under control, but Willie wasn't the best person in the world to be serving dinner to the guests. He poked his head through the open serving hatch. "Willie, come and give your Gran a hand. I'll serve in there."

It was getting on for eight o'clock. If everyone felt the effects of his Mother's laced coffee, by about ten o'clock the castle should be quiet enough for him to be able to deal with the girl and the Yankee.

Between courses he leaned against the serving hatch, discussing with the other two what had to be done. They spoke quietly, as though talking about everyday matters. "How you going to fix them, Dad?" Willie asked.

"I haven't worked it out yet, son." He paused to look round, making sure that no one was waiting to be served.

"I'd like to do the American."

There was so much hate in Willie's tone that his grandmother looked at him reprovingly. "Now, Willie, that isn't at all a nice thing to say."

"I owe him one, Gran."

"You leave it to your Father, there's a good boy."

"You going to use the bed, Dad?"

"Of course." Hogan sounded slightly shocked. "Its got to be done properly."

"And you're going to dump 'em in the loch?"

"Of course, son. We can't afford to waste good food for the fishes."

Hogan hastened forward to one of the tables with a basket of bread rolls. "Another roll, sir?" He waited, smiling, while the man selected one, then returned to the hatch. "It's the car I'm thinking about," he said quietly. "We'll have to dump that."

"Can I have the engine, Dad?"

"No, of course not."

"It's just what I want."

"Then you'll have to go without a bit longer." Exe's tone was sharp, and Willie subsided. "Tell me," Hogan went on, "did anyone see either of 'em just before dinner?"

"No."

"You're sure, Ma?"

"Positive, son."

"Good. Then here's what we do. Soon as we've prepared 'em for the trout, we'll take the Bentley and leave it up on the edge of Kelsie bog."

"Make it look as though they've gone down in it?" Mrs. Exe beamed approval. It wouldn't be the first time the bog had claimed a human victim, and as nothing ever came up from it again . . . ! One of the guests had finshed his course and Hogan hurried over to clear the plates and dishes from the table. Willie watched his father unhappily.

"Gran, what about all the work Selina does? I mean."

She took his hand and gripped it reassuringly. "Don't worry, lad. I'll see your Father puts an advert in the local paper for a replacement." She beamed at him. "We might find a nice girl. Someone you'd like."

Willie licked his thick lips. "Yeah. Yeah, I hadn't thought of that."

For the third time Jay passed through a doorway arch and found himself at the junction of two passages. Selina, coming up behind him, gave a wail of despair.

"It's hopeless! We'll *never* find our way out."

He secretly agreed with her. The cellars, passages and dungeon below the castle were a labyrinth. If he'd had any idea of direction at the start, he'd lost it a long time ago. Since the scare from the imitation skeleton his nerves had been taut. Normally, in a fairground tunnel, the incident would have been good for a small laugh, but down here in the cold, silently menacing darkness of the castle dungeons, it was unnerving.

It was all very well to tell oneself that it was a practical joke, the product of an immature mind, but that didn't do anything to ease the tension he was suffering.

"We'll try left again."

Selina gave a stifled shriek as a hangman's noose dropped from the blackness overhead to dangle in front of her face. She reeled back in fright, dropping her lantern which went out.

"Are you all right?"

"Yes. It—it didn't touch me—it was just the shock."

If Willie had been within reach, Jay would willingly have put the noose round the youth's neck and strangled him. The lantern Selina had dropped had fallen on its side and when Jay picked it up most of the paraffin had drained from it, but he managed to rekindle the wick. He

held the lamp out to her but she had her head tilted,
listening. The dangling noose was only inches from her face
but apparently she had forgotten it.

"Listen!" she said, clutching his arm. "What's that?"

He tensed, straining to hear, but all he could make out
was the sound of his own blood as it pounded through his
head, making a roaring noise.

"What is it?"

"I thought I heard someone about," she whispered.

Willie? Or Hogan Exe, screaming out a challenge? Jay
looked quickly at the luminous dial of his wrist-watch. The
time was getting on for half-past nine and it was a shock to
realize how long they had been in the dungeons already.
Assuming Exe to be back, would he set out to hunt them
down immediately?

Jay tried to force himself to think logically. Selina had
done splendidly, but lack of sleep the night before hadn't
done anything to help her stamina. Unless he got her out of
here soon, she would crack up. She was plucking at his
sleeve again.

"What are we going to do?"

"I don't know." It was perhaps best to be honest with
her. "Tell me, you know Willie better than I do. . . . Do you
reckon he'd put these booby-traps where he wanted someone
to go, or would he rig them up to keep anyone from straying
into a place he wanted to keep secret?"

"Secret?"

"Such as the way out, sweetheart."

"Oh!" Selina thought for a moment, then shook her head.
"I don't know," she confessed miserably.

"O.K., then we'll have to find out. . . . Come on."

They had moved less than ten yards down the dark
passage when a bloodcurdling shriek of maniacal laughter
split the silence, the noise echoing back and forth along
the granite corridor. Jay felt the hair rise on his scalp for a

moment until he realized that the lunatic caterwauling was coming from a loudspeaker mounted somewhere on the wall.

In a fury of rage he searched for and found the loudspeaker, tearing it from its bracket and smashing it to pieces on the stone floor, stamping hysterically on the thing until it was splintered beyond recognition.

When he looked at Selina she was weeping helplessly, her tears glistening in the light of the lantern as they ran unchecked down her face. She obviously couldn't take much more. Jay put an arm round her in a desperate effort to give what little comfort he could, but was overcome with weakness and pity as he felt the convulsive sobs that racked her small body.

Suddenly he lifted his head to listen. He shook her gently. "Ssh! " There it was again, a muffled noise that sounded like someone shouting. Was it still another of Willie's tricks? Or was it the bearded giant, trying to find them?

"Hey, there!"

It was plainer now, the voice so high-pitched that the question was almost a scream. *"What's going on! Please, what's going on?"* One thing was certain, Hogan could never have managed that tone, nor could Willie. There was another sound now, one that made him all the more uncertain, for it was like the rattling of chains.

"What is it?" Selina whispered frantically.

He shrugged, trying to interpret what the noises could mean. Then there was an unmistakable clatter: the noise of a w.c. being flushed. Jay was still bewildered when the rattle of the chains came again, then all was silent once more. A nightmarish quality had been added to the ordeal and he wondered for a moment whether he was going mad.

Move on, or go back? There was no dividend to be gained from the latter course and he dragged Selina forward, round a bend in the passage. They must have reached the end of the corridor for the walls receded, leaving black darkness in front of them. From the blackness a voice sobbed:

"For God's sake! What's happening!"

Selina froze, staring wildly into the darkness. "Who—who are you?"

"Is that you, Willie, playing tricks?" The words quavered with fear and suddenly Jay strode forward, holding the lantern high in order to illuminate as far ahead of him as he could. Then, dimly, he saw a patch of light in the darkness. Moments later Jay stared at the figure revealed by the light of a table-lamp: a thin man seated behind a huge desk.

"God Almighty! Have you come to rescue me?"

Charles White began to cackle with hysterical relief and he was screaming, beyond control, before Jay managed to reach him and slap him into silence.

In the bar, one solitary guest was broodingly contemplating his half-empty glass. "Quiet tonight," he complained to the shirt-sleeved Exe, who was leaning, arms folded, on the bar.

"Everyone decided on an early night," Hogan agreed. He regarded the guest in wonder, tinged with admiration; he'd drunk enough sleeping mixture for ten. Mrs. Exe, in full fig as Florence Nightingale, came through the back door of the bar carrying a candle-lantern which she put down carefully before looking inquiringly at her son.

"Mr. Neill's determined to make a night of it," he said loudly and admiringly. "Everyone else has gone to bed."

Mrs. Exe beamed fondly at Neill. "The only one up? Then I'll have to make you one of my special sleeping draughts, won't I? . . . What would you like?"

Neill smirked. "Whisky's my poison, Mrs. Exe."

"Then whisky your poison shall be," she said happily. "Hoagy, give Mr. Neill a drink on me."

"Right you are, Mother." He set about the task briskly.

189

She turned her back, lifting the lantern shoulder-high and opened its horn window. Hogan palmed the phial that she handed him from the lantern base, pouring the contents into the drink he was preparing.

Chapter Seventeen

JAY'S manner was firm as he shook his head. "It's no use; it'd need the key or an oxy-acetylene torch to get you free," he told White.

"You won't leave me!" The chained man was weeping. "If *he* comes down here, there's no means of telling what he'll do. He might kill me."

"He won't do that." Jay spoke irritably; appalled though he was by the man's plight, he was more concerned with the effect his story had had on Selina. She looked ready to collapse. "Do you know the way out?"

"No."

"Then we'll have to try our luck." He took the girl by the arm and more or less dragged her away, shutting his mind to the pleading cries with which White begged them to stay. "Come *on*," he hissed savagely at Selina.

"That poor man!" She was horror-stricken, gazing back over her shoulder as he pulled at her arm.

"There's nothing we can do, unless we find a way out."

Surely Exe must be searching for them too by now?

They passed through an archway and as they turned a corner, Jay pulled back in fear as an eye glared balefully at them out of the darkness. But there was no outcry, no violent rush to attack and he risked another peep round the corner. He felt a curious weakness as he recognized the object that had scared him. It was the glazed eye of a stuffed fish, mounted in a glass case!

He giggled, limp with relief, then sobered. "That must mean we're getting to a part that Exe uses regularly." He lifted the lantern high and could see, faintly the gleam of other glass cases, each one containing a monster trout.

Then the passage opened out into a chamber and here there was something else unusual.

In one corner there was a pile of rocks, each of them too big to be used as a weapon, some wire cages and what looked like a raised ramp. There was no time to examine the contents of the chamber; as soon as he had satisfied himself there was nothing that could be used to ward off an attack he moved on.

Ahead there was a further passage, with more glass cases hanging on the walls. He paid no attention to them until he heard Selina give a queer gurgling cry. She was staring at something, her face stiff with horror. *"Wh—wh—what's that!"* He raised the lantern.

A long oak plank was fastened along the wall. Someone had carved a row of crucifixes in the wood and under each cross there were some letters and figures. Jay stared in awful fascination at the carving nearest him. It bore the initials G.C. And the date—for the figures were dates—was yesterday's. There was no longer any doubt. Hogan Exe was a mass murderer, with seventeen victims to his discredit if the signs were to be believed.

"Come on," he said urgently, refusing to meet her questioning gaze.

A couple of yards farther on the passage bent at right angles and as he turned the corner he saw a sign: *Pass this at your peril!*

Immediately he moved beyond the sign something screamed at him from the wall. It was a luminous skull, set in a niche, and although the noise of it dinned through his head he was by now beyond feeling. This time Willie's trick made little impact.

"It's only another stupid trick!" he said mechanically as he hurried on. Suddenly the floor seemed to tilt and disappear from under his feet. He threw up his arms, his hands scrabbling wildly for something to hold, the lantern flying through the air and falling on the granite floor then rolling over the lip of the gap that had opened up.

Jay's wildly thrashing arms banged against the side of the passage as he fell, twisting and grabbing fiercely as he tried to stop himself following the plummeting light of the lamp that was spiralling downwards in the stone shaft until its light was extinguished, forty feet below, in the black water that gleamed momentarily as the lantern neared it.

His clutching fingers hooked on to a hold, his body banging painfully against the side of the shaft, as he clung on by his fingertips, and as the terrified girl cried out he called back, gasping: "Bring the light!"

She put the remaining lantern over the shaft, shuddering with terror at the spectacle of Jay. If his fingertip hold slid from the rim of the hole . . .!

He spared a glance downwards; it was a mistake: he had to close his eyes tight, then shake the sweat from his face. He had the strength to hold on for half a minute or so, no more. He looked down again, but there was no foothold to ease the intolerable strain on his arms; his only hope lay in their strength.

"Don't!"

She had reached down, sobbing, trying to grip his coat collar, but if she did that and he lost his hold, they'd both plunge to the water below. This wasn't just one of Willie's tricks: it must have been one of the original defences.

Selina shrank back at the fierceness of his command, staring down on him in agony. It seemed impossible that he should survive, but now he was putting his great strength to the test. Inch by inch his head rose as he pulled himself up. Now his head was above the level of the granite floor of the passage, but he couldn't do anything more. He had to lower himself, to rest his tiring muscles before another attempt.

"Please, how can I help?" she beseeched.

His voice was as calm as he could make it. "I'm going to try to get my left foot up to the floor," he gasped. "When

193

I try, grab me so I don't slip back." If once he had himself that high, he'd be able to get to safety with the help of his leg muscles to take part of the strain.

"All right."

She was being magnificent. Getting up she put the lantern down where it would be out of harm's way, then went back to the hole, lowering herself slowly and painfully to her bruised knees, crouching low in order to reach down as far as possible. Her fingertips were inches from her eyes.

"I'm ready when you are." Somehow her voice was level, although she didn't recognize the sound of it herself.

Again he raised himself, his biceps straining against the cloth of his coat until he felt that it must burst open. His hair was level with the passage floor, his eyebrows, his chin; face contorted with the strain. The most difficult part was yet to be attempted. Was it possible? It was now or never. "I'm . . . going . . . to . . . swing . . . my . . . leg . . . up. Try . . . to . . . grab . . . it . . .!"

He strove desperately to swing his body sideways to the right, then back to the left, raising his leg as he did so. Incredibly, he got his foot up and over the edge, but would have fallen back into the abyss had not Selina grabbed his coat collar and pulled with the strength of desperation.

It gave him sufficient purchase to be able to slide his left hand forward, so that it lay flat on the floor, enabling him to push himself up and roll forward away from the brink, his right hand groping blindly for another hold.

Selina cradled his sweat-drenched head in her arms, sobbing bitterly. "Thank God! Oh, thank God!" For a minute they lay huddled in each other's arms, trembling and weak with shock and terror. Gradually Jay recovered. He sat up, looking at the gaping hole.

"Master Willie didn't think that one up," he said shakily. "That's one of the ways the former owners used to dispose of their guests."

194

"Don't talk about it!" She was still clinging to him, shaking and distressed.

He held her close, staring over her shoulder. One thing was certain, they wouldn't be able to go on. They'd never be able to get across the gap. Even if they did, how many similar traps lay ahead? They wouldn't be able to take a single step without first testing if the going was safe.

"Selina, listen! We've got to turn back. Do you hear?" He shook her gently. "Do you understand?" He didn't seem able to make her realize what he was saying and he tried to lift her to her feet. He had just succeeded when the bass voice of Hogan Exe came booming through the passage.

"Are you there, Donaldson?"

Desperately, Jay clamped a hand over Selina's mouth. The sinister chuckling note of Hogan's voice had made her want to scream, but Jay stifled it. "Come on," he said urgently. "If we stay here, we're trapped."

Hogan stood and listened, head twisted to one side to catch any sound. He looked inquiringly at Mrs. Exe and Willie, who were standing silently, one either side of him, but they both shook their heads.

"Donaldson," he called again. "I'm coming to find you. . . . If you've hurt my niece . . . !" He waited for a moment, listening, then relaxed. The hunt through the vast underground network of passages and dungeons was a new and exciting experience. He was enjoying himself, for there wasn't the slightest chance that his quarry could escape.

He beckoned his son. "You take the east route, Willie. See if you can flush 'em out. I'll wait here for you to drive 'em to me."

Willie grinned. "O.K., Dad."

Hogan helped himself to a liberal swig from the flask he carried. "This isn't bad fun, Ma."

"I hope it won't take too long, dear. I've got the bread

to make for breakfast." She paused, considering her son's mood. "Hoagy," she said persuasively.

"Yes?"

"Wouldn't it be better to keep the American? You said it might be a good thing."

"He knows too much."

"Mr. White would like some company."

"Then we'll have to find him someone else."

"Mr. Donaldson's got a lot of money." She said it as persuasively as she knew how, but it didn't work.

"Mr. Donaldson's got a load of grief coming to him."

She accepted the inevitable. "If you say so, dear, although I would have liked a new fridge."

Jay wasn't sure whether he preferred the silence. If Exe kept calling out, at least it might be possible to avoid him, knowing where he was. But if the castle owner kept quiet they might blunder into him, for he'd see the light of the lamp they carried. Yet it was impossible to do without the lantern, especially after what had happened. Jay felt sweat break out all over his body at the mere thought of the deadly trap he had escaped—just.

There was an opening on the left. Had they passed it by when they were coming the other way? He didn't know. But if they kept straight on, that infernal shrieking skull would betray their presence. Barely hesitating, he turned and went into the new passageway.

It led into a small chamber, one that had an electric light bulb hanging suspended from the ceiling. Farther ahead there was something—something strange. Gulping nervously he crept forward and gaped when he found he was looking into a crude elevator, the door of which was slightly ajar.

He was filled with sudden wild hope. Just outside the door of the lift there was a switchboard. Controlling what? "If that thing works . . . !" He turned to the girl. "Where does it go to?"

"I've never seen it before."

"What the hell! So long as it works."

But it didn't.

He pushed the girl inside and followed her, pulling the door to and pressing the button inside. Nothing happened. There was only one button so there was nothing else to do to make the elevator ascend. Hurriedly he opened the door again and went to the switchboard. There were three switches and several press buttons on the board. He moved all the switches, pressed all the buttons, then got back into the elevator again. It had got to work this time.

He touched the button and the lift jerked into motion. He was flooded by a feeling of relief. It didn't matter where the lift rose to; at least they would emerge above ground-level. Of course, if Exe were waiting for them . . . ! Jay dismissed the thought, staring through the open side of the lift at the shaft through which they were rising.

It made him shudder with revulsion when he realized that the lift must have been put in the shaft that the original castle builders had constructed. He recalled Exe's tale of how the former owners had disposed of their enemies . . . the floor that tilted . . . the hole that opened up to allow their bodies to drop to the dungeons . . . !

The lift stopped. There was a door facing him and after a second's hesitation he opened it. But there was no attack, nothing but darkness, silence and *warmth*. He moved forward, lantern high, then gaped in disbelief. He was in his own bedroom!

His guns! Eagerly he hurried across to the light switch. "We're safe now! I've got——"

But the guns were missing. He searched frantically, but they were gone. Even the boxes of shotgun shells and the rifle ammunition had been taken. "Mrs. Exe!" He knew now the purpose of her visit to the room. She had been in it for only a few moments. She must have known beforehand where he had put the ammunition. They must have searched his room so often they knew where he put every item.

Sick with disappointment and filled with a cold rage against the Exes, Jay went over to the fireplace and picked up the stout, steel poker from the set of andirons. He hefted the thing in his hand; it wasn't the equal of a gun, but it was a deadly weapon for short-range work.

"The bed!"

He whirled round at her cry. Selina was standing in the middle of the room, one fist pressed against her mouth as she stared, wide-eyed, at the four-poster.

The bed was sinisterly different; each of the posts sticking out above the top of the bed, which was a couple of feet lower than normal. A threaded, steel column came down through the ceiling, the greased metal glinting in the light as it revolved, pushing down the padded top of the bed with smooth, silent, deadly and inexorable efficiency. He wiped the sudden sweat from his forehead.

"Wh—what is it?"

"The answer to a good many questions," he said grimly.

"What do you mean?"

"There's no time for that now."

Already it seemed as though they had been in the room an age, although it could not have been more than a minute. But once Exe found they had used the lift he would know where to look for them. Jay went to the door, switching out the lights and warning Selina to be quiet. When he opened the door there was not a sound to be heard.

There was sufficient light coming from round the bend of the corridor for him to see. The lantern was no longer useful and he left it, taking Selina by the wrist and leading her on tip-toe towards the bend. Once round the corner he would be able to see down into the great entrance-hall. If that was clear, so far so good.

He went down on hands and knees to peer through the carved balustrade. The hall was deserted and on the far side of it, as though beckoning to him, was the telephone booth. He inched back to whisper to the girl.

"I'll try to get to the phone."

"I'll come with you."

"No. Stay here." There was a vast expanse of open space to cover and once inside the booth he might find himself trapped.

"I'm going with you."

There was so much determination in the whispered words that he gave in. "All right. Come with me, but go to the door. If anything happens, get out and run for it."

Together they moved down the grand staircase, crouching and ready to retreat if necessary. But still the eerie silence continued. "What about waking the other guests?" Selina asked.

He shook his head. "It'd take too long to convince 'em. Besides, they haven't enough strength." Exe could have killed the lot of them together with one hand. Jay was at the foot of the stairs now, on the edge of the open space. Gripping the poker firmly, he straightened and began to sprint the fifteen or so yards to the phone booth, pushing the girl on towards the huge entrance-door.

The door of the booth creaked loudly as he opened it. He waited a moment, breathless, but no one seemed to have heard the din so he slipped into the box and lifted the receiver.

The telephone was dead.

Swearing, he ran to where the girl was standing. "They must have cut the line." He put out his hand to grasp the ornamental iron ring that was used to open the door. But although the ring turned, the door didn't budge. It was locked, and it would have needed an army tank to break it down.

He had taken it for granted the thing would be open. He had never known it to be locked. He cursed himself for being so stupid as to imagine that Exe would leave it as a means of escape, with the hunt on.

"The dining-room! " Selina whispered.

"We can get out there?"

"Possibly."

She led the way into the dining-room, hurrying and panting slightly in her haste. The windows were set high in the wall, but there was one that could be reached easily after they had carried a table across to it. Standing on the table, Jay took only a moment to open the window, which was fastened with a simple catch. The cold night air struck against his face as he put his head out and tried to see the ground below.

But the wall was too thick. He had to scramble into the embrasure before he saw the ground, about ten feet down. The snag was that the rock finished almost underneath the window. Beyond it was a drop to the surface of the loch. Anyone dropping from the window stood a good chance of missing their footing and plunging into the black water.

"I'll go first," he said.

But she clung to his arm. "You might break your neck! "

"If I don't, I'll like as not get it broken for me."

"All right," she said helplessly. At any second she expected to hear Willie's hateful voice in her ear, to cringe at his mad, cackling laugh. She shuddered, putting the idea from her and watching Jay apprehensively as he shuffled into the embrasure as far as he could, preparing himself for the jump that would land him safely on the rock below.

A mist was starting to rise from the loch and it didn't make Jay's judgment any easier. But it was now or never. His knees were flexed, his feet as firmly planted as he could manage. The poker in his left hand was a hindrance and he threw it down first, wincing at the clatter it made. Then he launched himself into the darkness, landing heavily and pitching forward on to his face.

A second later he was scrambling up, the only damage a few scratches on his hands where he had used them to save

200

himself. He turned and looked up at the window. Selina's face was no more than a white blur above him. "Come on. Just jump. It's quite simple."

Selina closed her eyes and leaped towards him, trusting him to catch her. She landed short of where he had fallen and he had to reach forward to grab her as she staggered on the uneven ground. But then they were safely together, panting and breathless, but safe.

He released her and fumbled round for the poker until his fingers closed over it. It wouldn't be more than a couple of minutes now before they were able to get away. He led the girl at a crouching run, across the front of the castle towards the lean-to. Once they could get into the Bentley . . .!

But the Bentley failed to respond to the starter. Sick with apprehension, Jay got out of the car and opened the bonnet. A moment later his fears were realized. The distributor cap was off; the rotor arm missing. All the other cars in the lean-to had been dealt with in the same way.

Chapter Eighteen

WILLIE came back, white-faced. "They've used the lift, Dad." "They couldn't have found it," he said savagely.

"Honest, Dad."

Hogan looked at his son for a long, tense moment. "They couldn't have found it if the door was shut."

"Oh, dear!" Mrs. Exe looked at them both in turn. "I *might* have left it open when I brought the guns down."

"Did you?"

"Did I what, Hoagy?"

"Did you leave the door open?"

"I really don't know, dear."

He could have smashed his fist into her stupid face, but he controlled himself. The inquest could come later. "If they get away . . .!" He turned and began to run, the other two stumbling after him as well as they could manage.

When he reached the kitchen he began to switch on every light, examined the windows and then went into the hall which sprang into vivid relief as he touched each of the switches. It was when he rushed into the dining-room that he saw what he feared he would. The embrasure window was open.

He sprinted back to his office, reaching it just as Willie arrived there. Hogan grabbed the walking-stick that was really a disguised rifle and stuffed a handful of rounds into his pocket, issuing orders as he did so. "Willie, take the car down to the road. They can't have been gone too long. You know what to do if you see them." He glared at the youth. "Well, go on, move!"

Mrs. Exe came puffing into the office and looked apprehensively at the rifle. "Is that going to be necessary, son

202

You know I don't like violence."

"I won't use it unless I have to." He looked round. "Where's that damned torch?" He found it in the second drawer he searched and now he was ready. He hurried out of the office and into and across the entrance-hall, moving with incredible speed and silence for his size.

Jay dragged Selina down behind one of the cars just in time as Willie came panting into the lean-to. Before the American could decide what to do, the youth switched on the headlamps of the shooting-brake. Jay crouched lower, feeling his heart bumping with apprehension. He couldn't attack Willie now; it would mean launching himself into the dazzling beams of the lights. He would be fully illuminated and too blinded to see his enemy.

Then the shooting-brake's engine roared into life and he heard the bonnet being slammed down. A moment later Willie drove off at a furious pace, the spinning wheels sending a shower of gravel into the air. Jay breathed a prayer of thankfulness that he had resisted the impulse to run when he had seen some of the castle windows light up. He and the girl would have been trapped in the beams of Willie's headlamps.

Crouching, grasping the poker in his right hand, Jay ran forward, avoiding the noisy gravel and keeping to the freshly-dug flowerbeds against the castle wall. At the corner he dropped to his knees, risking a peep with his head almost at ground-level. His caution was justified. Outside the open door of the castle, huge and menacing in the light streaming through the open door, Hogan Exe was standing.

The noise of the car's engine had faded now and it was obvious that Exe was listening, turning his head from side to side. Jay felt the girl touch his leg and turned round to motion her to silence before peering round the corner again to watch Exe.

If the big man came towards them Jay would have to try

an ambush. Exe seemed to have a weapon of some sort, possibly an iron bar, so it would be poker versus bar of iron. The American could feel the moisture on his fingers, where he was grasping the metal of the poker. He took the thing in his other hand and attempted to wipe his right hand free from sweat. If it became too slippery it would be useless.

After what seemed an hour, Hogan moved. He sprinted *away* from the watcher and Jay sighed in relief. The hotel owner was probably going to check that all the boats were tied up at the tiny landing stage that was built alongside the loch.

The temptation to run was almost irresistible, but he controlled it, trying to forget his own apprehension in giving comfort to the girl who was crouched near his legs, trembling and exhausted. He heard the sound of quick footsteps on gravel, then saw vaguely, in the light from the open doorway, Hogan Exe running swiftly down the drive.

Sudden hope flooded the fugitive. He turned to whisper to Selina. "We've got to get to a boat."

She scrambled to her feet, but he held her back, listening. Hogan was lost in the darkness; the sound of his running feet had faded. He might be a hundred yards away; he might be returning silently, hoping to flush his quarry. If anything was going to be done, it had to be done at once. To reach the rowing-boat they would have to pass before the castle and be silhouetted by the light coming from the open doorway. If Hogan was looking towards the castle when they did that, he'd be able to see them even if he was a quarter of a mile away.

But the risk had to be taken.

"Ready?"

She gulped, nodding wordlessly. He sensed, rather than saw the movement and took her hand. "O.K. Let's go."

He moved at a deliberate pace, heading for the far corner of the castle, terribly conscious of its bulk looming menacingly up on his left. No sound, no shout indicated that they had been seen, but now they were approaching the open door. It seemed a mile across, the lights brighter than gala illuminations.

Jay took a deep breath. "Come on."

Now he and the girl were outlined; if Hogan was looking in this direction . . . ? But they moved into the comparative darkness, no longer an obvious target, and he ran on, pulling her along as he stumbled over the uneven earth, blundering into bushes he had never realized existed.

The mist on the water was thickening, with visibility no more than a few yards. He thrilled with relief as he saw the dim outline of the small landing stage. Quickly he bundled the girl into the nearest boat and was about to climb aboard himself when he stopped to listen.

The silence was absolute. Now that they were down at the level of the water all sounds would be muffled by the mist, but if Hogan had been coming down the rocky slope to the boats Jay couldn't have failed to hear him. Satisfied, he took the two minutes it occupied him to untie all the other boats, handing the lines to the girl.

"Grab hold!"

Getting the oars into the rowlocks made enough noise to attract half Scotland, or so it seemed. But then he had the blades dipped into the water and after only half a dozen strokes he could no longer see the rocky shoreline, or the vague dark mass of Aarolie Castle. Hogan couldn't find them in the mist, even if he had a boat at his disposal. "Relax, we're safe enough now."

"You mean that?"

"Sure I do." Confidence was flowing back into his mind, fresh strength returning to his body. He rowed vigorously, moving the boat through the water at a good speed until he judged he was at least two hundred yards from the landing stage. He rested his oars. "You can drop those lines now." The boats wouldn't drift back to shore; they'd have to be collected from another boat, or by someone swimming.

Selina forced her numbed fingers open, letting the ropes fall away. Their roughness had torn the skin on the palms of her hands and they were sticky with blood. Not that she cared. Now that her companion had made the announcement that they were safe she was transformed. Even to breathe the misty loch air, and just to know that she was alive and maybe had a future, was an exhilarating experience.

But Jay had been too optimistic. While he had rested on his oars the boat could have turned round. There was no landmark, no star by which he could check in which direction he was facing. The surrounding mist might keep them safe from observation, but there was a loss to balance the gain. If he started rowing again he might, for all he knew, be heading straight back to the castle.

He peered round anxiously, trying to find something— anything—that would give him a fix for navigation, but there was nothing but the white mist surrounding them. He made a few tentative strokes with the oars, but still there was nothing. "Goddam! "

"What is it?"

"Nothing. . . . Get some rest." Was it imagination, or had he felt the slightest puff of wind on his right cheek? . . . Yes, there it was again, stronger this time and it made the mist swirl. It happened again and this time it was almost a breeze. He had seen the terrifying swiftness with which the weather could change on the loch. Maybe this was going to be another instance.

He was right.

Within a matter of seconds the mist was thinning as the wind increased in strength. He was twisting in his seat, looking out over the bows when he caught his breath. Immediately in front of the boat, and no more than fifty yards ahead, he could see a patch of starry sky, against which was outlined the grey mass of the castle. The very thing he feared, had happened.

But now there was a star by which he could steer. If he could turn the boat, then keep the star directly over the stern . . . ! He dipped the blades deep in the water and strained at the task of getting away from the castle. Half a minute later there was a splintering crash and the boat tilted, then dipped alarmingly.

Selina couldn't check a cry of alarm as the boat seemed about to capsize, but somehow it righted itself and settled steadily. Jay turned, trying to make out what had occurred. It was simple enough. He had rammed the bows of their boat smack into one of the others, catching it broadside, splintering a hole big enough to sink it. Their own boat was undamaged, but the noise of the collision *must* have been heard by Exe.

It had.

At first Hogan had been puzzled by the sound, then he realized what must have caused it. At top speed he ran to the landing stage, to find all the boats gone. The mist was thinning, a wind springing up. He stared at the sky. Was there a suspicion of light in the east? Dawn was not far off.

He listened intently and could just make out the sound of oars splashing in the water. Suddenly he began to laugh, the noise booming out over the water. His whole body was shaken by mirth and then the spasm ceased abruptly, cut off in a split second.

He turned and began to run up the sloping rock path, round the front of the castle and to the lean-to. From his pocket he took the Bentley's rotor arm and replaced it. Half a minute later he was driving the silver-grey convertible madly down the drive, without using lights.

As he reached the road he saw Willie, standing crouched beside the shooting-brake that was blocking the exit. Willie straightened and ran up to him, frightened. "What's happened?"

"We've got 'em boy, we've got 'em."

The hotel owner might have been discussing some

marauding rodents they had managed to trap. His manner was calm and it had its effect on the youth.

"They're out on the loch," Hogan said. "He's bound to row over to the other side and when they get there I'll be waiting. . . . I'll take the shooting-brake and head them off. You take this Bentley and leave it just by the edge of the bog. You know where I mean." He chuckled. "It'll be just another tragic accident. Holidaymaker and local waitress walking into a bog . . .!' "

Willie nodded approval. "You think of everything, Dad."

Exe climbed out of Donaldson's car and went across to the shooting-brake, putting his gun on the front seat and climbing behind the wheel. A few seconds later he had manœuvred the vehicle on to the road. He went roaring off with Willie following more slowly in the Bentley.

The mist had all gone and it was nearly full daylight by the time Jay reached the other side of the loch. He steered for the place from which he had fished. "There's a path leading back to the road."

Selina looked ahead, past his shoulder. There was no sign of a track, just a little open space on the shore that was hemmed in by cliffs of granite. "You're sure?"

"Tam Bruce came along it one day. He'd got his bicycle with him."

The bow of the boat rammed the rock shelf and the American pulled the boat alongside so that Selina could climb ashore. A minute later they were scrambling up the steeply shelving rock. "There it is!" Jay pointed to the faint track that was revealed where a large pocket of earth offered a softer surface. The path led upwards to and over a ridge of granite and when he topped the rise Jay stood for a moment to study the lie of the land.

To the left rose the bare slope of the mountain that formed one side of the glen. Ahead, the country was wild and broken; hard going even for deer. Fortunately, to the right it was easier. The ground there was fairly level, with a ridge of rocks a mile or so farther on. From his rough estimate, the road must run on the other side of the ridge.

For a moment he turned to stare back, across the water of the loch to the castle, a grim, grey pile in the distance. Had Exe given up the search and cleared out? Or was the hunt still on?

"What are we waiting for?" Selina was shivering in the chill of the morning air. He took off his jacket and placed it round her shoulders.

"I'm just having a looking to see which is the easiest way," he lied smoothly. So far as he could make out there was not a single movement in the whole, vast expanse that was spread out before him, but in that countryside an army could have been in ambush. "O.K. . . . Come on."

He held out his hand to the girl. She was in poor shape, white-faced, her blonde hair hanging loose and matted. She was trembling with fatigue, but she did her best to keep pace with him, stumbling along without making any complaint. They were moving downhill and what had looked to be smooth enough ground from the ridge was now revealed as rough going, the gorse thickening and tearing at their clothes. Had he missed the way? Certainly he was on some sort of path, but was it the right one?

Then the track forked; neither side appeared to be more worn than the other. Selina brushed her forearm wearily across her face. "Which one do we take?"

"The left one, I think."

The sharp ridge of rocks ahead still looked to be the same distance away. On the left there was a cleft; maybe a track led through it, which would save climbing the ridge. But it would also be likely that Exe would come through the ravine, if he was still hunting for them.

"Do you know this part of the country?"

She shook her head. "I've never had time to explore it. There are some bogs, though. I do know that. Bad ones."

209

"Where?"

"I don't——" Her eyes widened in surprise as Jay staggered, but before she could speak the sound of a shot smacked across the gorse-covered land. Jay had dropped to the ground, a hand clasped to his left arm, just below the shoulder. Horrified, she saw the bright red blood start to seep through his fingers.

"Get down!"

She dropped to her knees beside him. "You're hurt! "

"It's nothing. . . . A scratch." It was true, the bullet had done no more than gash him, but the real hurt came from the realization that he had been out-generalled. The shot had come from *behind* him. What a damned idiot he had been standing there, presenting himself and the girl as easy targets!

"Let me see." She prised his fingers away from his arm despite his protests, and examined the wound while he turned his head to try and see where their enemy was. The damage to the flesh was slight, but it was bleeding freely. She felt in the pocket of his jacket and found a clean handkerchief which she folded into a pad.

"Hold this against it."

He did as he was told, automatically pressing the linen against the torn flesh, as he still tried to locate Exe. But it was hopeless. "Come on." Crouching, he moved off along the left-hand track, gaining what shelter he could from the gorse and any irregularity in the ground.

It was a tiring method of travel; before he had gone three hundred yards he would have given a great deal in order to be able to stand upright and stretch. Not until he had gone a little farther did he realize he was doing the wrong thing. So long as they stuck to the path, Exe would have no difficulty in following them.

"We'll turn off the track the moment I see a likely spot," he whispered. His arm was beginning to hurt; he knew that before long he would be too exhausted to go any farther.

Selina, too, was in bad shape, her mouth gaping as she tried to draw air into her lungs.

Ahead and to his right there was a possible place to hide. The gorse was thicker there, the bushes forming a screen. If they went *round* the bushes, they could lie in concealment until Exe had gone past. The bearded man had the advantage of knowing every inch of the terrain; would he spot their move?

Jay nodded his head to indicate the place to make for. "Over there."

Quietly, trying not to make a sound, they crawled round the edge of the gorse, dropping behind it when they were concealed from any possible sighting from the track. Selina began to sob noiselessly and hopelessly. Jay longed to comfort her, but could do nothing more than touch her hair as he listened with desperate concentration for the sound of movement. But when he did hear something, it made his blood run chill.

Exe was close, and laughing.

The laugh ceased abruptly and then Hogan spoke. "Get out of there, you rotten capitalist! "

Selina looked up at the wounded man in terror, but he cautioned her into silence with a finger to his lips. Exe was much nearer than Jay had guessed, but he was probably trying a bluff. He couldn't know where they were.

"I can see you." Hogan's tone was conversational. He couldn't have been more than thirty or forty yards away at the most. Jay put his arm across the girl, pinning her down motionless.

"You think I can't see you?" There was a short pause. "All right, I'll prove it."

This time the sound of the shot and the strike of the bullet were simultaneous. The projectile hit the bare granite not a foot away from Jay's head, then went spanging away into the distance as the first echoes came drumming back from the mountains.

Jay scrambled forward in panic. To get back on the path seemed to be the only thing left. Exe must know exactly where they had tried to conceal themselves, and it was probably only because the fiend wanted to prolong the torture that they were still alive.

There were some loose flakes of rock underfoot and Jay picked one up, using his uninjured arm to sling it as far as possible to the right. The trick worked; there was the explosion of sound from another rifle-shot and he took advantage of the echoes that came back from the mountains for what seemed like half a minute. Under cover of them and the alarm cries of some birds, he forced the girl to move on round the edge of the patch of thick gorse, pushing her back to the path.

It was possible to make some sort of speed there and by a miracle no more bullets were fired.

Selina was stumbling along in a daze by this time, barely conscious, her face, legs and arms scratched cruelly by the gorse needles, the skirt of her dress in tatters. If he had loosed his hold on her she would have fallen and not got to her feet again. But some reserve of strength, a passionate desire to stay alive, drove the American on although it seemed so hopeless. Exe could surely move up as soon as he wanted and dispose of them both.

Once again Jay was bitterly aware of the mistake he had made. He should have told the girl to go ahead, while she was still capable of making it. Then he could have waited for Exe, or gone running off in another direction, drawing Exe off and doing the madman out of one quarry. That way Selina at least would have been saved. Now it was all no good.

Selina dropped suddenly to her knees. "I can't go on," her head drooped, her hair falling over her face so that he had to stoop down beside her to hear what she was whispering. "Leave me. Save yourself."

He tried to pull her up. "Come on, it's not far now." He

212

risked taking a glance at the ridge of granite ahead and felt a surge of fresh hope when he saw that he was right. The ravine that ate into the ridge was only yards further on.

"Come on, we're almost there!" He helped her to struggle to her feet.

Even when they reached the road they wouldn't be safe, though. Very few vehicles passed along it at any time of the day, but at least it was a symbol of hope. He thought he knew what was in Exe's mind. The big man intended to let them get within a few yards of comparative safety, then he'd shoot—and this time to kill.

There was one slim chance. "Listen," he whispered urgently, "I reckon I've got this figured out. When we get near the road we'll go to ground again——" He stopped, looking at the track ahead with dismay. It was plainly marked here and it turned left, straggling up the far side of the ridge, passing over open ground.

If they moved along it any farther they'd be without the cover of a blade of grass. Exe would be able to pick them off as he wished.

Straight ahead a small burn flowed down from the other side of the ravine, its bed littered with boulders. If they could follow its course, would it lead them to the road? A dozen such streams passed under tiny bridges every mile or so and there was no way of telling whether this was one of those that flowed under the road he knew.

"Come on!"

In the tiny pause, Selina had sunk to her knees again and this time he couldn't get her to rise. There was only one alternative to abandoning her. He would have to carry her.

Trying to get her slung over his right shoulder was a desperate business. He had to use his left hand to help and the movement of the arm opened the bullet wound again causing fresh blood to flow down his arm, resoaking the caked sleeve of his shirt. With the girl hanging limp and

213

unconscious over his shoulder, he stumbled on, expecting to feel the hammer-blow of a bullet at any moment.

But then he saw the open terrain ahead. He had passed through the ravine and reached the edge of a stretch of bright green, level ground with no cover. The area was like an amphitheatre, with the high rock encircling it and no way out other than by turning back, or going straight across to where there was another ravine. Either they would have to reach that escape route, or climb the almost sheer rocks that surrounded the place.

He hesitated for a moment. How far behind was Exe? Surely he would arrive at the edge of the open space before Jay could cross it? If he did, he'd be able to shoot them down like trapped animals. But to wait was fatal and the American started off after a last, desperate glance along the way he had just come. There was no sign of Exe and Jay moved out into the open.

It was an agonizing effort to keep straight on without stopping to look back. Even now Exe might be lining up his rifle sights . . . ! Jay plodded on, the weight of the girl's limb body increasing with every step he took. The scene before him blurred and he tripped, almost dropping her. but recovering just in time. He was moving slowly now, almost spent, and it was this that saved him.

The ground seemed to collapse under his foot as he put it down and he fell, losing his grip on the girl for a moment as he plunged face down into what he had taken to be mossy ground. But already his body was soaked with slime and he felt himself starting to sink. He knew the truth then: he had walked straight into one of the bogs Selina had mentioned earlier.

It clutched at him with inexorable strength, but he managed to struggle his way back to firm ground. When he found purchase he stretched out to the pull the girl to safety. He could just get a grip on one of her wrists and he tugged in an excess of fear. Her body had sunk in two or three inches already and he sobbed with the effort to get her free.

The cold wetness of the quagmire brought her round and with the realization of what was happening to her she screamed, starting a blind struggle the only effect of which was to make her sink more quickly.

"Selina! For God's sake, lie still!"

He was supporting himself by his injured arm and had almost lost his grip on her before the words penetrated her panic. She quietened, her blue eyes staring at him wildly imploring, all the more vivid in the midst of the dark green slime that covered her face.

"Lie still! "

She did as she was told, lying rigid as he braced himself for another effort. The veins in his temples stood out in the stress of it. Then, with a disgusting gurgle, the bog released its grip and he pulled her, weeping desolately, to the solid ground.

"Good show, old man!"

The ironic words echoed round the amphitheatre and Jay lifted his head wearily to see Exe standing on the slope of the ravine, laughing gleefully. It was the worst moment of the whole dreadful nightmare. Selina, covered in the foul stinking mud of the bog, was beyond caring, sobbing helplessly, and he himself hadn't the strength left to stand.

Even if he could have fled, there was nowhere to go. What made it all so bitter was the realization that they had been driven into the situation by Exe, who had manipulated their movements as though he was a puppet master and they were his dolls. He was filled with impotent rage against the brute who had taken away their dignity in such a cruel way. He glared at the madman with hatred as Exe called out again.

"Say good-bye to her, Donaldson, but don't take all day over it. I've got to go and see to breakfast." Hogan tilted his head back and bellowed with laughter. "But I can't go and do that until I've put you two to bed."

Jay watched the bearded man raise his gun and braced himself for the impact of the bullet. But when the shot rang out he wasn't hit. The bullet struck the ground a yard to his right: Exe was still enjoying tormenting them.

"I'm sorry, Donaldson, but the next one'll have to be aimed at you. I'm getting a bit low on ammunition." Exe raised the gun again.

"Exe!"

The bearded man whirled to stare in disbelief at the uniformed policeman who had suddenly appeared. Tam Bruce was higher up, on the top of the rock ridge and Hogan reacted swiftly. The shot he had intended for the American was aimed at Bruce. The policeman dropped and for a moment Exe thought he had hit the man, but then Bruce's voice rang out from where he had taken cover.

"Don't be a fool, man. Gi' up. I'm no' alone."

It was a bluff, a stupid bluff. Exe whipped the cartridge case out of the rifle and inserted another shell. This time he wouldn't miss. But then two other uniformed figures appeared, some distance from where Bruce was, and the bearded man took a snap shot at one of them. It was good shooting. Exe saw the puff of dust that rose from the impact of the bullet which hit the policeman in the middle of the chest. The man was probably dead before his body fell on to the rock.

Hogan screamed in wild joy. "I'll kill you all. . . . The lot of you." But when his fingers searched for another round of ammunition, they found nothing. Frantically he fumbled in all his pockets, but he had used every round he'd brought with him. Raging, he threw the useless weapon at Bruce, who had risen and was watching warily.

"It's no use, Exe."

"Go to hell!"

Hogan knew only one thing: he had lost. Immediately he knew another fact—they would never take him alive. He turned and began to rush down the steep, rocky slope, moving with incredible speed, heading for the level arena-like surface below.

Bruce realized what was going to happen and gave a shout. "Dinna do it, man!"

But Exe couldn't have heard the words. If he did, he paid no attention. He was pounding across the earth like an Olympic sprinter and even if the policemen had been down on the level ground with him, they'd never have been able to catch him.

For a dreadful moment Jay thought that the crazed man was coming to wreak vengeance on the girl and himself with his bare hands. But Exe's glaring eyes were staring at something else beyond. Now Jay realized what was going to happen and struggled up on to his knees, clasping Selina's head against himself to protect her from the terrible sight.

Exe, his mouth wide open, his mighty chest labouring from the strain, was almost at the edge of the bog now. Five yards, three, one. He was going at full pelt when he jumped, to land at least seven yards inside the rim of the quagmire. His huge body smashed down into the green slime with a sickening, dull splash. As he hit the surface of the bog he began to scream.

The screams had died away by the time Bruce and his fellow constable reached the edge of the bog. Only Exe's head was above the surface now and he glared at the two officers in silent hatred, his wide eyes terrible in the contorted face as he went under.

"And I thought it was the poachers firing!" Bruce whispered in anguish.

Jay was propped up in the hospital bed, leafing miserably through a pile of illustrated magazines, when the severe-looking nurse entered the private room he occupied. "Constable Bruce to see you, Mr. Donaldson," she said with professional briskness.

The solemn-faced Bruce tiptoed in as though in the presence of death, his face even more serious than Jay remembered. "Well, Mr. Bruce?"

"You're well, yoursel', Mr. Donaldson?"

"I'll be out of here tomorrow."

"That's braw news." He seated himself carefully on the edge of the chair Jay indicated. "The Inspector thought you'd like to be knowing what's going on." He shook his head regretfully.

"I feel I'm to blame for your hurts, and that's a fact. I knew the Exes were using too much wire. Drums and drums of it they were buying. Then it occurred to me they were using it to trap the salmon. When I thought of that, I got reinforcements, ye ken, and while we were searching for the nets, we heard the shooting . . . !" He sighed. "Dreadful mistakes I made, sir. Dreadful." Poor Jamie MacLean, shot dead by Exe, and only in uniform one month. Terrible."

"You didn't make any bigger mistakes than I did, Mr. Bruce."

"Aye, but with me it was a matter of profession, sir." His voice saddened. "That's what counts. A man has to be guid in his professional status, if you follow my meaning."

Jay wasn't interested, but the constable wasn't going to be put off easily. "The Inspector will be along to take a statement. It's a big, awfu' business this. They were all in it. All of them."

It was hardly news. "You've arrested the others?"

"Aye." Bruce brightened. "That Mrs. Exe! Offered to take over the cooking at the prison! What a woman!" He had at last found something that impressed him, but her grandson wasn't in the same category. "Wullie'd got a watch on him when we arrested him. A watch that had belonged to a Hugh Hamilton—a mannie listed as missing a short while back. . . . Hamilton's car was found at Renniton Moor, about forty miles away. We thought he'd gone in one of the bogs there—Renniton's a gey dangerous place.

218

"But Exe must have smothered him in that bed. And many another too." He swallowed. "The Inspector's got divers working in the loch. Mrs. Exe told them where to look. I dinna think she knows how serious her position is. . . ." He sighed. "Sixteen, seventeen murders! Och, we'll be famous."

Although Bruce appeared to face the prospect with some pleasure, there was little or no joy in life for Jay. The shock was wearing off and his bodily hurts were healing well enough, but the thought that he had been mixed up with a mad family—a bunch of homicidal maniacs—depressed and saddened him. Bruce was regarding him oddly, a peculiar expression on his face.

"Miss Lester will no doubt be very grateful, sir," he said archly.

"Miss Lester?" He didn't know the name.

Tam Bruce seemed very slow in answering. "Miss Lester, sir? You don't . . . ? I'm talking about Miss Selina Lester, Mr. Donaldson."

Lester? He had always assumed her name to be Exe. He had once asked her what her surname was, he recalled, but she had given an evasive reply. Suddenly he shot upright. "You don't mean . . . ?"

Bruce was even slower to answer, but at last he relented. "Miss Selina's no' related to the Exes, sir. At least, only by marriage. There's no blood tie, ye ken?"

"You're *sure*, man?" It was terribly important.

"Oh, aye." Bruce smirked complacently. "I made a few inquiries. She's as sane as I am. . . . Or as you are," he added generously.

"Damn you, Bruce!" Jay grinned, throwing back the sheets and jumping out of bed. Bruce helped him don a dressing-gown. The policeman was still solemn-faced as he regarded the eager man.

"The lassie's in the last room on the left, sir. Turn right and it's the last on the left."

Jay's eyes glinted as he contemplated the man's blank expression. "Bruce, you're a friend for life. I love you."

He opened the door and rushed into the corridor, following the instructions Tam had given him. The first door on his left was open and he glanced into the room as he passed. Inside, sitting up in bed with a huge tray of chocolates, sweets and fruits, was Charles White, too intent on selecting another chocolate to notice the American pass his door.

Now Jay was at the end of the short corridor, outside the closed door that hid the one person in all the world he wished most to see. For a moment he braced himself, running the fingers of one hand through his curly hair in an effort to make it tidier. Then, shoulders squared, he knocked on the door.

The severe-looking nurse opened it and regarded him with immediate suspicion and growing hostility. But over her shoulder he could see Selina, propped up in bed with her shining hair tumbling round her shoulders. She was wearing something blue tied with ribbons and looked too beautiful to be real.

"Out! "

"Mr. Donaldson! " the nurse began indignantly. "Go back to——"

He reached out, grabbing her by the shoulder. "Out, out, *out!*" He gave her bottom a hearty slap to help her on her way, then closed the door, turning to gaze at the girl who was regarding, him wide-eyed with dawning hope.

"Ah, Miss Lester! There's something I want to ask you."

He strode across to the bed, wrapping his good arm round her as she clung to him and started to weep happily.